# BEYOND DEFEAT
*An Epilogue to an Era*

This edition of *Beyond Defeat,* limited to 1000 copies, is published with the kind permission of Ellen Glasgow's literary executors, Irita Van Doren and Frank V. Morley.

# BEYOND DEFEAT

*An Epilogue to an Era*

BY

ELLEN GLASGOW

EDITED

WITH AN INTRODUCTION

BY

Luther Y. Gore

THE UNIVERSITY PRESS OF VIRGINIA
*Charlottesville*

THE UNIVERSITY PRESS OF VIRGINIA
*First published 1966*

This edition is limited to 1000 copies

69/5412

Library of Congress Catalog Card Number: 66–28520
*Printed in the United States of America*

# ACKNOWLEDGMENTS

For their considerable aid, grateful acknowledgment is made to friends at the University of Virginia: Oliver L. Steele, of the Division of Humanities; Floyd Stovall and James B. Colvert, of the English Department; and John C. Wyllie, Librarian of the Alderman Library.

LUTHER Y. GORE

*Charlottesville, Virginia*
*April 26, 1966*

# CONTENTS

# INTRODUCTION

## I

FOR over three years after the publication of *In This Our Life* in 1941, Ellen Glasgow worked on a sequel to that novel and finally completed sometime in January, 1944, the third draft of a small book which she named *Beyond Defeat*. She undertook this task largely because she felt her readers had missed the point of *In This Our Life*.

After completing *Beyond Defeat*, she worked for the next three months with Frank V. Morley and Irita Van Doren of Harcourt, Brace and Company, making minor revisions to the work and settling plans for format and binding. Then, quite suddenly, she changed her mind and decided not to publish the sequel. For many months she never even mentioned the work in her correspondence. Once, in November, 1944, when she had less than a year to live, she wrote to Morley, asking whether he, too, felt the decision not to publish had been wise.[1] Except for that brief inquiry, however, she apparently had managed to put the little book out of her mind.

The decision not to publish *Beyond Defeat* was probably well taken on Ellen Glasgow's part. A slim novelette of only 151 typewritten pages, the work is, as the subtitle indicates, an epilogue rather than a new story. As such, it could not have been read by itself, and it would have been inaccessible to any reader not already familiar with *In This Our Life*. Then, too, the book said explicitly what Ellen Glasgow had hoped *In This*

---

[1] This letter is owned by Harcourt, Brace and World, Inc. The unpublished letters owned by this publisher will hereafter be identified as Harcourt, Brace and World.

*Our Life* would convey subtly and artfully. Even her heartfelt desire to make the message of *In This Our Life* clear could not prompt her to weaken the integrity of an earlier work by publishing another story to explain it. Finally, not the least of all her likely reasons for canceling publication may have been the realization that *Beyond Defeat*, though it has many fine qualities, falls short of the high standards set by her best work.

Still, the somewhat summary decision not to publish belies the seriousness with which she had pursued the composition of *Beyond Defeat* during the three years of its evolution. She felt from the beginning that she had excellent reasons for writing such a work. Although *In This Our Life* had received high praise and won its author the Pulitzer Prize, it had been mistakenly identified as a book that exploited the degeneracy of Southern life and advanced a hopelessly pessimistic outlook on life in general. Some critics took the novel to task for its "pessimism," but even those who praised it seemed to miss the point. Only one reviewer, an anonymous critic in *Time*, perceived that *In This Our Life* was really not about defeat. He saw rightly "that the major theme of *I.T.O.L.* is that 'tragedy is never in defeat but in surrender.' "[2] Such had been the burden of all the work of Ellen Glasgow's mature period, and it must have galled her that this last work, which had belatedly won her such wide public recognition, was being praised highly and condemned widely on the wrong grounds.

Some indication of the degree of concern she felt was her hurried attempt to publish an explication of *In This Our Life* soon after the Pulitzer Prize was announced in May, 1942. She wrote to Donald Brace on May 9, 1942, only four days after the announcement to ask his help in placing her own commentary

[2] Letter to Helen Taylor, March 28, 1941, *Letters of Ellen Glasgow*, ed. Blair Rouse (New York: Harcourt, Brace and Co., 1958), p. 282. Subsequent references to this collection will be cited as *Letters*.

on the work in the *Saturday Review of Literature*.[3] The commentary was never published there, but her essay was reworked later to become the chapter on *In This Our Life* in *A Certain Measure*, published a year later in the fall of 1943. This chapter shows that she was chagrined by the widespread misunderstanding of her intentions in *In This Our Life* and hoped to correct it in a sequel which she had already named *Beyond Defeat*.

She had this idea, however, even earlier than May, 1942, the time of the Pulitzer Prize. James Branch Cabell, her long-time friend and the fellow writer who had read *In This Our Life* and made comments and suggestions on it, had written to her in December, 1941, some six months before the Pulitzer Prize, exhorting her to "hie to Lavinia's bedside" as, apparently, she was about to do.[4] This suggests that Ellen Glasgow had already returned to her story (Lavinia is the wife of Asa Timberlake, the hero of *In This Our Life*) to compose the epilogue, *Beyond Defeat*. A still more convincing argument for this early inception of *Beyond Defeat* is a letter from Marjorie Kinnan Rawlings of January 17, 1942, telling Ellen Glasgow that "Mr. Cabell says that you are considering following Roy and Stanley a little further"[5] (Roy and Stanley are the two daughters of Asa and Lavinia Timberlake).

Whatever the date of its beginning, the sequel to *In This Our Life* had advanced far enough by February, 1942, for its author to begin writing her publisher about it. By that time she knew at least what the theme would be and had a rough notion of the book's length.[6]

[3] *Letters*, p. 296.

[4] This letter is in the Ellen Glasgow Collection in the Alderman Library at the University of Virginia. Subsequently, this collection will be identified as U. Va.

[5] Letter at U. Va.

[6] Letter at Harcourt, Brace and World.

In the months that followed, she worked assiduously and produced a first draft early in May, 1943. Donald Brace, her publisher, encouraged her, as did many of her friends such as Cabell, Bessie Zaban Jones, Van Wyck Brooks, and Marjorie Kinnan Rawlings. For her own part, Ellen Glasgow was doubtful about the success of the work. Ill health and a feeling of depression over the tragic events of World War II sapped both her energy and her enthusiasm. At times writing became almost impossible, as she confided to Van Wyck Brooks in a letter July 27, 1943, for pains in her back allowed her to type only a few minutes a day.[7]

Despite these burdens and the task of preparing A *Certain Measure* for publication in the fall of 1943, she managed three full drafts of *Beyond Defeat*. There is every indication that she pursued the writing of her sequel to *In This Our Life* with the same devotion and care that she had expended on all the other work of her mature period. Her last work, though never published, had clearly been a labor of love for her art, and a labor perhaps more demanding than any she had undertaken before.

In view of the difficulties imposed on her by her ill health, her depression over the war, and the task of working simultaneously on two books, it is surprising that Ellen Glasgow had such a clear conception of the job she had undertaken and could work out the technical problems of the sequel as well as she did.

What her readers had most misunderstood about *In This Our Life* was the ending of the novel, the point to which the story brings the lives of the principal characters, Asa and Roy Timberlake. Asa, it must have appeared to her readers, was doomed to final failure, to the disappointment of his life's

[7] *Letters*, p. 327.

dream of leaving his hypochondriac and domineering wife Lavinia for the peace and fulfillment of Kate Oliver's farm. Roy, in desperation over Craig Fleming's rejection of her in favor of her sister Stanley, had taken the final leap to disaster in her night's folly in the arms of a stranger she met in a bus stop as she fled from the family house. On the surface, at least, all was lost by Asa and Roy to the forces of darkness and chaos.

To Ellen Glasgow, however, all was not lost. Stripped of financial independence, love and understanding, and even gratitude in the long, sad history of his life, Asa still had self-respect and a keen ironic wit with which to fight off temptations to self-pity and abject submission to defeat. Most important, he had hope, dim as it might be, as the last paragraph of *In This Our Life* shows: "Looking up at the closed sky, once again he had a vision of Kate and the harvested fields and the broad river. Still ahead, and within sight, but just out of reach, and always a little farther away, fading, but not ever disappearing, was freedom."

Ellen Glasgow believed that readers were judging both Asa and Roy by standards too much like those of Lavinia and her wealthy uncle William Fitzroy. They seemed to miss the subtle point that nothing external was needed to complete the nobility of Asa and of his daughter Roy, so much like him—that hope against odds and the determination never to knuckle under were the greatest of virtues and very much their own reward. As Ellen Glasgow had conceived *In This Our Life*, even the sort of "external" rewards for fortitude such as those she had granted her heroines in *Barren Ground* and *Vein of Iron* were unnecessary for Asa and Roy Timberlake.

Clearly, however, such rewards were necessary if the value of fortitude—"the vein of iron"—in Asa and Roy was to be correctly seen by unsubtle readers. And this suggests what must have been the first major decision about the story of *Beyond Defeat*, that some means of externalizing that virtue should be found.

For Asa, the means were inherent in *In This Our Life*, namely, for him to leave Lavinia and join Kate Oliver on her farm. This is what happens in *Beyond Defeat*. But Ellen Glasgow does not easily grant this bit of poetic justice. Even though Asa can leave Lavinia financially independent because of the annuity William Fitzroy has left her (Fitzroy's death from cancer is anticipated in *In This Our Life*), Asa breaks with Lavinia conscious that he has violated the still sacred trust of marriage. This is what he seems to mean, in part, at the end of *Beyond Defeat* when he says that Lavinia has won "the last battle."

As regards Roy, the task of externalizing the rewards for hope and the triumph of character over circumstances must have been more difficult. At any rate the solution that the author hits upon seems less satisfactory. She finds it necessary to make Roy pregnant as a result of the one night spent with the young Englishman. This cliché of plotting suggests a faltering in imagination. But the birth of Timothy is only a part of the continuation of Roy's story, only a part of the further heaping upon the heroine of tribulations that will bend her down to the point of breaking. Ellen Glasgow has Roy fall ill of pneumonia and then, apparently, of tuberculosis. Finally, Roy is threatened with losing Timothy to strangers, when Lavinia and Roy's Aunt Charlotte refuse to take care of the boy. All this apparently is done to make Roy's triumph over life all the more admirable, for despite these hardships she does not break, but resolves to go on "beyond defeat," hopefully to recover her health, her child, and perhaps even her former fiancé Craig Fleming.

Roy's tribulations begin to lift from her shoulders when Kate

Oliver agrees to keep Timothy on her farm while Roy under-goes treatment for tuberculosis. This part of the plot does not come as a surprise, for Kate's genuine goodness has been ade-quately prepared for both in the earlier novel and in the sec-tions of *Beyond Defeat* which precede this turning point in the story. Kate's decision, furthermore, reinforces an important theme of *In This Our Life*—the value of simple kindness and selfless concern for others. Still, this appears almost too easy a way out of the dilemma Roy faces. One feels that her triumph has arisen not from within but from outside the fortitude she inherited from Asa.

The story of *Beyond Defeat* does not end with Asa's and Roy's beginnings on the road to happiness, though it was the main purpose of the sequel to place them there. Continuing with her concern for social history, Ellen Glasgow has Lavinia die at the end of *Beyond Defeat* as a means of signifying the end of an era in Virginia, perhaps in the South. This death was unnecessary for the clarification of the themes of *In This Our Life*, however much it may fit in with the social history. At best the death seems gratuitous, at worst a naïve kind of poetic justice.

Even though the plot of *Beyond Defeat* reveals some weak-ening of the author's established skill in the manipulation of events, the action of the book shows an attempt at the kind of organic unity with other elements of the work that Ellen Glas-gow felt was important to successful fiction. Throughout the sequel there is a good deal of emphasis on the theme of self-reliance, and the book is full of devices to reinforce this theme by the idea of "circularity," the coming back to the self. We see it symbolically in the circling flights of birds, for example. And there are references to the "return to the self" in Craig's dialogue and Roy's interior monologue. The action supports the theme in Roy's return to Queenborough and in the final return to Lavinia's house at the end of the book. The skill of the author in weaving symbol, action, and dialogue around her theme is in itself a solid indication of the endurance of her art despite the terrific hardships under which she was forced to work in the closing months of her career.

Ellen Glasgow seems to have decided that characterization in *Beyond Defeat* would remain very much the same as in *In This Our Life*. Since she was concentrating on the destinies of Asa and Roy, which seemed to give readers the most trouble, she could, of course, leave out some of the characters of the earlier work. Stanley's destiny (her marriage to a Hollywood producer) is only mentioned in *Beyond Defeat*. Andrew Timberlake is recalled merely in passing, Parry Clay and his family are never brought up, and William Fitzroy has died in the interval between the time of the two books, a space of roughly three years.

Of the characters Ellen Glasgow retained, Lavinia is most like herself in the earlier work. The author's skill in delineating this hypochondriacal, hypercritical, selfish, and domineering figure suffers no diminution in the sequel. Aunt Charlotte Fitzroy is made to assume a more important part in *Beyond Defeat* than she had had in *In This Our Life*. She has been changed from the agreeable but ineffectual figure of the earlier work to a fairly convincing spokesman for the older, dying generation, a generation which had descended to the level of caricature in Lavinia in *In This Our Life*. Charlotte has become selfish and somewhat hypocritical in the sequel, but it is clear that the characterization is well under control. Charlotte, the first to meet Roy upon her return from New York, also serves as a convenient listener while Roy narrates what has happened to her in the intervening years, and she provides an economical way of giving the reader the details of the Timberlake family history over the same period of time.

Roy and Asa are most changed from the earlier characterizations in *In This Our Life*. Asa has lost almost all his wit and humorous detachment. On Kate Oliver's farm he seems strangely complacent and almost selfish. Roy has lost most of her dash and vigor and now has tendencies to self-pity only vaguely hinted at in *In This Our Life*. Neither father nor daughter seems as attractive in their ultimate success as they were in the failure they experienced in the earlier work. All this may have been intentional on Ellen Glasgow's part. Certainly Roy's experiences in New York were of a kind to dampen the strongest spirit. And Asa, in his years of worrying over Roy, the only one of his children he really loved, may have seen the sharp edges of his ironic wit worn away.

Craig Fleming, who was not very successfully characterized in *In This Our Life*, is again rather lifeless. His almost convincing liberalism in the earlier work has degenerated into something akin to war-poster patriotism. Kate Oliver, on the other hand, who played a minor role in *In This Our Life*, assumes a much more important role in the sequel. She becomes a convincing embodiment of the "simple goodness" Craig claims for her, but she is never maudlin in the role. The characterization of the child Timothy, who is, perhaps, somewhat precocious for his age, is nevertheless a respectable performance.

Despite the moderate success of the characterization in *Beyond Defeat*, there is a lack of movement, a pace at times altogether too slow, throughout the work. Ellen Glasgow may have felt the need not only to "externalize" the rewards for fortitude in her main characters, but also to make clear by overt explanation the message she felt she had failed to convey to her readers in *In This Our Life*. The interior monologue, carried on mostly by means of indirect quotation, is her usual method of expounding the meanings of her characters' experiences, and she uses it often in *Beyond Defeat* to explain her ideas about fortitude. She may have gone too far with the device, however, because the lengthy speculations of Roy and Asa are a chief factor in the lack of vitality in the sequel. The interior monologue is used in *Beyond Defeat* more than in any of her other works. But the function the sequel was to serve—the clarification of the theme of *In This Our Life*—may account for, if not justify, her heavy reliance here on this device.

*Beyond Defeat* is bound quite closely in its themes to *In This Our Life*. In addition to the theme of fortitude, certain subsidiary themes of the earlier work are developed. We find at least some continued concern for the dying away of the old era of the South and the passage into the new. The death of Lavinia, which the author acknowledged was allegorical,[8] and the description of the skyline and the war workers' homes in Queenborough remind us of the fading away of the old, aristocratic way of life with its cruel and sometimes hypercritical moral code. Before us rises the new day of crowded urban-industrial life and the encroachment of international involvement on the easy, isolated life of the city. Some readers, as Ellen Glasgow noted in *A Certain Measure*, failed to perceive that in *In This Our Life* she was writing about much more than a single family; and it was probably her purpose in *Beyond Defeat*, therefore, to expand the meaning of her work beyond the Timberlake family to convey something about the whole era. This theme, however, is subservient to the author's primary concern for the value of fortitude, and, if anything, the sequel establishes less universality than the earlier work, despite Craig's and Asa's comments on World War II.

The style of *Beyond Defeat* differs from that of the earlier work. *In This Our Life* is marked throughout by a clipped, rapid style, one fairly close to the modern spoken idiom. Images of speed and noise abound. This style is modified exten-

[8] *Letters*, p. 340.

sively, however, to suit the author's new purposes in *Beyond Defeat*, and the language is noticeably subdued. There is a certain mellowness about it, especially in the latter portions of the work. Movement is slow and meditative. Images of slowly circling birds and of the quiet, dignified decay of Hunter's Fare, Kate Oliver's farm, help establish this atmosphere. On the whole, the style is well adapted to the nature of the work and it shows to advantage Ellen Glasgow's mastery of the materials of her craft.

## II

The manuscript material now in the Glasgow Collection in the library of the University of Virginia includes a set of notes for *Beyond Defeat*, three complete drafts of the novelette, and a number of pages of states of various parts of the text. These manuscripts, consisting of more than 500 pages from which came the final text of 151 typewritten pages, constitute a remarkably complete gathering of the materials associated with a book. These documents, more complete than anything else in the Glasgow collection, make it possible to trace closely the evolution of the work and to gain important insights into Ellen Glasgow's working methods.

The earliest materials, the rough notes, include among other things a page of "Possible Titles." This was probably some of the earliest writing, because an interoffice memo at Harcourt, Brace and Company records that the title *Beyond Defeat* had definitely been settled on as early as February, 1942. The list of titles is of interest primarily because it establishes that Ellen Glasgow had chosen a theme for the work at a very early date. The "possible titles" follow:

AFTER THE END: AN EPILOGUE TO A LIFE

AFTER DEFEAT: AN EPILOGUE TO A LIFE

These titles suggest that she was considering the idea of continuing both the story of Asa and Roy and the theme of the dying tradition of the aristocratic South. It is also interesting to note that one title, "Do We Always Return?: An Epilogue to a Life," appears in the first sentence of the novelette. As readers of her letters, *The Woman Within,* and *A Certain Measure* know, once she had found a phrase to express something that caught her fancy, Ellen Glasgow was prone to hang on to it.

The other notes include bits of dialogue, character description, interior monologue associated with the central theme of the book, and descriptions of Kate Oliver's farm, Hunter's Fare. These notes are dated throughout the period from October 9 to October 27, 1942, and apparently they were made during visits to friends at Willow Hill, a plantation on the James, and at the famous James River plantation, Berkeley. These descriptions conform so closely to the real plantations that it is obvious they provided the models for Hunter's Fare, though the plantation in the novelette is considerably more run-down than either of the two real life estates.

One bit of description in the notes is of particular interest: "As the light changed, the [scarlet] burning torch of the green-tree [caught fire and] blazed [in the] by the river's edge." This appears later, almost intact, in the text of the narrative. During her visit to the James River, Ellen Glasgow was struck by the remarkable beauty of a tree seen against the sunlight and she decided that it would be an appropriate image of renewed hope in her novelette. The three drafts show that she first intended the image to be associated with Asa's "triumph," his escape to Hunter's Fare. Then she decided to apply it to Roy's "internal victory," and finally she changed her mind again and placed it in its ultimate location where it reinforces Roy's feeling of elation over Craig's thinly veiled proposal of marriage. Ellen Glasgow must have felt drawn to the image from the first, and the only question in her mind was where it would fit most appropriately in the text.

The descriptive notes for the novelette point up the fact, established by the author herself in numerous comments about her work, that she was writing about a part of Virginia's social and cultural history at the same time that she was dealing with universals. These notes show that the accuracy of the setting was important to her. They reveal, too, that even in the earliest stages of her work Ellen Glasgow was concerned with style. The notes were considerably "worried over" in phrasing, and some words and phrases were subjected to as many as two or three revisions even at this early stage.

How much of what she observed in the world around her which does not appear in these notes but eventually made its way into the novelette we cannot know, of course. But there is evidence that it may have been a considerable amount. Wartime Queenborough in the last part of Beyond Defeat is very close to the Richmond of that day. And the author's concern for the position of the humanities in wartime almost certainly was inspired by an article by Henry Seidel Canby in the Saturday Review of Literature, January 16, 1943, and by correspondence with Bessie Zaban Jones,[9] whose husband, Howard Mumford Jones, had expressed a similar concern at the time. The observations about maternity wards may have come from corre-

---

[9] Letters, p. 308.

spondence with Mrs. Jones,[10] as did the ideas about homes for refugees, mentioned in a letter from Mrs. Jones.[11] The account in *Beyond Defeat* of Roy's diphtheria is remarkably like Ellen Glasgow's earlier description of a childhood illness in *The Woman Within*.[12] In these ways, at least, her own life and thoughts provided material for the world of her fiction in *Beyond Defeat*.

The actual composition of *Beyond Defeat* involved the writing of three complete drafts of the text. This had been Ellen Glasgow's practice since *Barren Ground* (1925), as she explained in *A Certain Measure* and *The Woman Within*. The first draft, begun probably in December, 1942, is a 132-page typewritten manuscript identified by a penciled note in the author's hand as "Very Rough Outline." The note is somewhat misleading, for the draft is far from an "outline." Though made almost unintelligible in parts by copious interlineations and deletions of words, this draft is, nevertheless, a complete version of the story with all dialogue and description fully realized. In addition to the text itself, there are nine pages of early states of various parts of this draft. Apparently they were discarded in the process of composition.

This draft has revisions made in type, in ink, and in both blue and black pencil. While these different media do not necessarily indicate separate revisions of the work, they prove that even in her earliest drafts Ellen Glasgow was concerned about achieving a satisfactory style. She was always concerned, as she maintained, with making her style "a natural part of the organism, not . . . extraneous decoration."[13]

[10] *Ibid.*, p. 302.

[11] October 19, 1942, at U. Va.

[12] New York: Harcourt, Brace and Co., 1954, pp. 87–88. Both in turn recall a passage in *Virginia* (1913).

[13] *A Certain Measure* (New York: Harcourt, Brace and Co., 1943), p. 176.

In *A Certain Measure*, she claims her first drafts were written "for balance of structure, vitality of characterization, and in the effort to capture and hold a sustaining mood."[14] The first draft of *Beyond Defeat*, at least, will bear this out. The "balance of structure" (by which I assume she meant the working out of the plot and the relative emphasis to be given parts of the story) and the characterization and mood of the first draft are retained in both succeeding versions. In *The Woman Within*, moreover, she maintains that "vitality and vividness of theme" were a concern in her initial drafts.[15] This, too, is borne out by *Beyond Defeat*: the first draft sets the theme for both later drafts. In the second, the passages of interior monologue which overtly expound the theme are made more vivid and forceful, but the essentials are all in the first draft.

The descriptions of Queenborough and of Hunter's Fare are revised most heavily in the first draft itself. Dialogue is the least "worried over" part of the composition at this point. This is natural, I think. The maintenance of a "sustaining mood" demanded a very precise choice of words in the descriptions. The dialogue, however, may have given her less trouble simply because she was already familiar enough with the characters to know the "voice" each would have.

Composition of the first draft of *Beyond Defeat* took until late April or early May, 1943. There is no indication how long the second draft took, though by early January, 1944, the third and final draft had been finished and sent off to the publisher.

The second draft is a manuscript of 130 pages. An additional twenty-two pages of states of various parts, composed after the completion of the first draft, may also be associated with the composition of the second and grouped with it.

[14] Page 262.
[15] Page 286.

The second draft is a much cleaner copy than the first. There are only 10 or 15 per cent as many interlineations and deletions. A good deal of the revision between the first and second draft apparently took place "silently"; that is, the author simply made changes from the first draft in her head and then typed them out in the second draft. On the manuscript itself, corrections or revisions again are in type and in pen and pencil. They appear on all but two pages. Some pages are revised only slightly; others have interlineations over as many as half the lines.

In *A Certain Measure*, Ellen Glasgow claimed her second drafts were written "for the sake of atmosphere and the arrangement of scene and detail."[16] Many of the differences between the first and the second draft do affect tone. The second shows much attention to muted colors and slow, rising motions, as in the descriptions of the pigeons in Queenborough and the crows at Hunter's Fare.

In "arrangement of scene and detail" there are many minor differences between the first and second draft. A few fairly long passages in the first draft are moved to new locations in the second, and there is a good deal of deletion and addition of minor details of description, dialogue, and interior monologue, involving often only a word but sometimes phrases or whole sentences.

The third draft, completed in early January, 1944, is a manuscript of 151 typewritten pages. The greater length of this draft is due solely to wider margins on all sides. There are also twenty pages of states of various parts of the text composed and discarded somewhere between this draft and the second one.

The third, as we would expect, is the cleanest of all the drafts. Some crossing out and interlineation with the typewriter is evident, but these changes seldom exceed two lines. As in the

[16] Page 262.

other drafts, there are revisions also in both pencil and ink. The most heavily revised part of the third draft is in the last chapter of Part III. On February 5, 1944, Ellen Glasgow asked Frank Morley to send this section back to her for further correction after she had sent him the third draft.[17]

Her concern in writing third drafts of her work was "an austere perfection of style."[18] The third draft of *Beyond Defeat* bears this out, for it is mainly minor matters of expression, rather than the story, characterization, or theme, that receive attention here. She made at least one revision which Frank Morley suggested in a letter of February 3, 1944, after he read over the manuscript.[19] Morley objected to the fact that by the time Roy and Asa get back to Queenborough after hearing of Lavinia's death from Aunt Charlotte, the florist has already managed to deliver "a spray of mourning flowers." This seemed too quick to Morley. Ellen Glasgow accordingly removed the spray from the Timberlake door. She was not so amenable to Morley's further suggestion that the fresh lipstick Kate Oliver kept for visitors was an implausible accommodation even for Kate Oliver. The lipstick remained for Roy to use when she got ready for supper at Hunter's Fare.

The three drafts of *Beyond Defeat* provide a complete demonstration of the evolutionary process of Ellen Glasgow's novels and reveal that her own comments on her working methods do not exaggerate the systematic way she went about her work. Taken together with what she wrote about her craft in *A Certain Measure* and *The Woman Within,* the three drafts confirm a most workmanlike approach.

Although she undertook a particular job of revision in each draft, there are numerous other revisions of various elements

[17] Letter at Harcourt, Brace and World.
[18] *A Certain Measure*, p. 262.
[19] Letter at U. Va.

throughout the whole course of the composition. These additional revisions are instructive because they reveal both the complexity of even so slight a work as *Beyond Defeat*, the author's keen awareness of the problems involved, and her good judgment in solving them.

## III

While the characterizations in *Beyond Defeat* were built on those of *In This Our Life*, some changes were made which may be explained by events that have happened to the characters during the time between the end of the action in the novel and its resumption in the novelette. Evidently Ellen Glasgow had planned from the first that Roy would appear considerably more sober in the sequel than in *In This Our Life*. Roy's ironic sense of humor is notably diminished in the sequel. Here she is worried and appears almost a petulant creature at times. But that the author intended this is strongly suggested by the revisions of the descriptions of Roy and of her dialogue throughout the course of the composition. All the drafts contain, for example, revisions of Roy's dialogue to expand contractions, even when they would have been most plausible, to give her speech a somewhat more elevated tone. Such phrases as "Why on earth," "You angel" (addressing Charlotte), and "under the sun" (in "I might be any age under the sun") are deleted, perhaps because they show a too talkative and vivacious character. In addition, the author revised a few passages that suggested Roy's former sense of irony. When Asa jokingly asserts that what Lavinia wants is to have her husband back and to keep her grievance at the same time, Roy replies, "How can you laugh?" in a line added in the second draft. When Charlotte wants to know how Roy could have given herself to the young Englishman, the second draft reads: " 'I know,' Roy answered, with her old mocking smile. 'But it was possible. Anything is possible to any kind of people.' " The phrase, "with her old mocking smile," is omitted in the third draft.

Charlotte Fitzroy, now the widow of William Fitzroy from *In This Our Life*, must have presented at least some minor problems of characterization. The revisions throughout the drafts seem to indicate a lack of sureness on the author's part. The problem was to convert a fairly inconspicuous character from *In This Our Life* to one of the two chief spokesmen in *Beyond Defeat* for the dying aristocratic tradition. It would not do to make just another Lavinia. And it would not do to exaggerate or otherwise distort what little we know of Charlotte's character from *In This Our Life*. When Ellen Glasgow first wrote *Beyond Defeat*, apparently she thought she had hit just the right balance between credibility and caricature in the portrayal. But as she worked on the novelette she must have come to feel that there had been too much of the comic in her first attempts at Charlotte. The revisions show the deletion of many passages that might suggest comic garrulousness. In the second draft, for instance, she revised the following simply by dropping the third sentence: "Is it really you, Roy? Why didn't you write to us? I wonder why Lavinia will keep this hall so dark." When Ellen Glasgow typed the second draft, she removed a long passage in which Charlotte rambles on about cruelty, the Bible, and her husband's "plain language." In another place, a long digression by Charlotte on Lavinia's heart ailment is excised.

Some other revisions of Charlotte's characterization are merely changes in diction aimed toward more refined speech. For example, "movies" becomes "romantic motion pictures" and "fun" becomes "pleasure." These changes are, of course, consistent with the "Victorian idiom" a woman like Charlotte would have used.

Of all the characterizations in the book, that of Lavinia seems most firmly set from the beginning. There are fewer changes in it than in any of the others throughout the drafts. In some places, Lavinia's addresses to Roy, "my dear" or "my child," are deleted, possibly because their inclusion would have made Lavinia's hypocrisy too pointed. Occasionally her diction is elevated by changes such as "in Queenborough" to "on James River" (whereby Lavinia seems to associate herself with the aristocracy even more) and "illegitimate child" (referring to Timothy) to "a child born out of marriage."

The characterization of Asa Timberlake, like that of Lavinia, undergoes little change throughout the various drafts. Unlike the characterization of Roy, which was made increasingly sober in the revisions, Asa's is modified in the rewriting with the apparent intention of restoring to him some of the mellow irony which characterized him in *In This Our Life*. In one passage, "he was smiling now" is added to his description, as was the sentence, "There was a whimsical overtone in his serious voice," no doubt to show that Asa could still take his troubles with a grain of the salt of irony. One deletion made during the typing of the second draft softens Asa's reaction to Roy's return to what we would expect from the father in *In This Our Life*. The deleted passage is: "When you went out into that storm, you rushed into a pack of trouble, my dear daughter." Finally, when Asa reaches the Timberlake home in Queenborough, he is made to say in the early versions, "At last I am free!" In the third draft this passage, which reveals a rather undesirable side of his character, is deleted.

No significant revisions were made in the characterizations of Kate Oliver and Craig Fleming. Timothy, however, was subjected to many revisions, possibly because Ellen Glasgow was introducing a new character for whom there were no precedents in *In This Our Life*, but also because she was unsure, from her own limited experience, how a small child would speak and act. Frank Morley complimented her on her achievement in Timothy, though he did find, he said, one place where Timothy's voice did not ring true for a child of his age. Unfortunately, Morley did not say where he felt the false note occurred.

Timothy's speech is revised in many places in the various drafts of the work to make it more believable for a child of two and a half. For example, "Bird" in numerous places in the first draft becomes "Birdie" in the second. "My bird!" becomes "Mine! Birdie!" In the first draft, Timothy says "Ise Timmy . . . Roy'll," but this is revised in the second to "Timmy . . . Roy'l." In the same way, "I'm hungry, Mamma" becomes first "Timmy's hung'y," then finally "Hung'y."

The characterization of Timothy plays an important part in the symbolism of the book, and certain additions made by the author from time to time apparently were intended to strengthen this function. In the second draft, for example, the assertion that Timothy's glance is "as gay as the song of a bluebird" is added along with Roy's thought that Timothy looks "like a hungry robin" while he eats. These additions help to establish associations between Timothy and the birds in the story, the pigeons and crows, which introduce a motif of freedom that runs counter to the oppressive bonds of tradition so prevalent in Queenborough, especially in the Timberlake home. The passage in which Craig comments on the meaning of Timothy's name was also added during the second draft.

Revisions of the themes throughout the composition take the form mainly of revisions of dialogue or of interior monologue and authorial comment. There are many such revisions. Their number is understandable, I think, because it had been the themes of *In This Our Life* that unsubtle readers had misunderstood and that the sequel was written to clarify.

These revisions affect both the main theme—that of "fortitude"—and the many minor themes, some of which had been evident in Ellen Glasgow's work almost from the first.

The addition of the line, "Yes, it was all the same, yet how different" to the second draft at the point where Roy is looking at the skyline of Queenborough, reinforces the idea that the self has an identity in part independent of the external world. The meaning here, of course, is that though the external world has remained essentially the same, the person viewing it has undergone profound changes in her way of seeing things. In the second draft, also, the following lines appear for the first time: "In death, and in death alone is there finality," and "Then I tell myself the end may be easier than the beginning." Both passages forward the central theme of the book and they make fairly straightforward statements. They are intended, apparently, to rectify misinterpretations of *In This Our Life*. Another passage in the first draft, related to the main theme of the work but possibly capable of creating misunderstanding, was simply omitted from the second draft. Craig is speaking to Roy: "The trouble with you is you're too strong," he said. "It is the strong who suffer most in the world. If you'd given way before this, everything would have come right for you." This passage states an implied contradiction of the main theme and it also suggests an inflexibility on Roy's part. Neither implication was desirable, and the author was wise to omit the passage altogether.

An attack on sentimentality, so often a part of Ellen Glasgow's works, also appears in *Beyond Defeat* in the assertion that pity ruined the worlds of Roy and Craig. Though put in Charlotte's mouth, the statement must be taken seriously as one of Ellen Glasgow's own observations because it reiterates a theme found in many of her earlier works. This clarification of thematic focus was introduced in the second draft of the novelette.

Other minor thematic elements were taken out of the work at a fairly early stage. For example, in the first draft Asa comments at some length on the rise of fascism and communism, and at another point he speaks about the delusion of an anthropomorphic God. Both these passages are omitted in the subsequent drafts.

One matter having to do with the themes was omitted, apparently at the last moment, from the third draft. The words "toward that dead past which had rejected the future" are deleted after "hand" in the passage "then suddenly, he stretched out his small hand." This deletion is hard to explain because the passage as it originally stood made quite clear some of the symbolism of the work. Perhaps Ellen Glasgow felt it was simply too explicit; yet there remains a good deal of other "explication" (viz., Timothy as the "unknown future" and "the storm without" as a reflection of "the storm within") that is allowed to stand. Why she should suddenly decide to be more subtle in this case is beyond speculation. The symbolic "explication" of Timothy's holding out his hand to the dead Lavinia closely reflects the author's own interpretation of the novelette in a letter to Frank Morley.[20]

The "rough notes" for *Beyond Defeat* document Ellen Glasgow's concern for a realistic, probable setting for her story. In the three drafts this concern arises continually in the form of the revision of factual details in the background and action. The author was concerned, naturally, that factual matters in *Beyond Defeat* be consistent with corresponding details in *In This Our Life*, and she tried as always to make the background and action reinforce the particular atmosphere she was seeking to convey.

Her care for these matters in reflected in the fact that nearly every detail involving numerical quantity is revised at least once. For instance, Lavinia's age is given first as "sixty-three"

[20] December 7, 1943, *Letters*, p. 340.

and then revised to "sixty-five" in the first draft itself. Kate Oliver's age is revised, too, from "fifty-five" to "fifty" in that draft. Stanley's marriage to the Hollywood producer takes place first "a few months" after she arrived in California, then "a few weeks afterward." In the first draft Craig is to report to the navy "the next day," but the second draft reads the "next week," a change which makes his meeting with Roy somewhat less coincidental.

A number of the revisions of factual matters were intended to create a more probable action. Some of these involve only a few words. The meat the young nurse will feed Timothy is a "lamb-chop" at first, then it is a mashed-up "cutlet," and, finally, some "ground hamburger." The child is to be served "tea" at Hunter's Fare at first, but this is revised, in the second draft, to "milk." Crag is said in the first draft to have tried to volunteer for the navy in October, 1940, but this is subsequently changed to "before Pearl Harbor," a revision probably intended to make Craig's idealism somewhat more believable. A date as early as 1940 would have made little sense. I have spoken already of Morley's suggestion of revising the business about the funeral spray. Another matter connected with the exact time of Lavinia's death involved the revision of the final draft to show that Lavinia died not "hours ago," but "soon after we reached you" (referring to Charlotte's phone call to Asa at Hunter's Fare).

The "arrangement of scene and detail," the important concern in the second of the three-stage progress of Ellen Glasgow's work, is one of the most interesting aspects of the evolution of Beyond Defeat. I take "arrangement" to mean setting a passage in its most dramatic or logical place in the narrative. So many passages were relocated throughout the course of the composition of Beyond Defeat that this work must have been a major part of her task.

The shifting in the rough notes of the "gum tree" image to its ultimate, most effective position is but one example. There are many other such changes. In the first state of page one the first paragraph is a description of the Timberlake house in Queenborough, and the second is Roy's interior monologue in which she asks herself if one always returns to the place where he has suffered most. In the next state, however, the order of these two paragraphs is reversed, possibly to introduce more immediately some of the major themes and to establish what I have called the circular pattern of the book by advancing the idea of the "return" in the first sentence of the first page.

Sometimes the relocated passages are fairly long ones. One passage of twenty-four lines was moved from its place in the first draft to a position four pages earlier in the second. This section includes Roy's admission to Charlotte that Timothy is her baby and the account of the circumstances of his conception. The passage was moved because it makes more sense to have Roy explain these things to Charlotte when she first asks about them, rather than some four pages later in the narrative.

While many passages were relocated during the course of composition, others were simply deleted, usually because they slowed the action or introduced motifs superfluous to the themes of the narrative. These deletions vary in length from a single sentence to units several paragraphs long. Altogether about thirty such passages were discarded at one time or another during the composition, mostly between the first and second drafts.

A typical example is related to the point in the story where Timothy is eating his lunch. In the first draft the nurse says, "There's a fine, tender chop all ready for him in the twinkling of an eye." Presumably this reminds the precocious Timothy of the children's song "Billy Boy," and he blurts out "Cherry pie!" whereupon the nurse compliments Roy on the child's knowledge of Mother Goose. This part of the scene is omitted in the second draft.

Another, longer passage, also omitted in the typing of the second draft, describes Roy and Asa as they take the station wagon to a garage for repair. There a "thoughtful stranger," much like the stranger who helps Roy and Timothy onto the bus to Hunter's Fare, picks them up in his car and drives them to the Timberlake house in Queenborough. This episode was wisely omitted because it slows the action and suggests an undesirable lack of concern on Asa's part for his ill wife.

Later, between the second and third drafts, a number of relatively short passages were deleted. For example, when she is speaking of the doctor in New York who is making arrangements for her treatment in a sanatorium, Roy explains that "he has something to do with the management. It wouldn't cost me anything but my railroad fare." This passage was omitted possibly because it raised puzzling questions about how Roy's treatment was to be financed; perhaps the suggestion that it would be free struck a wrong note for the author. Another short passage also omitted from the third draft is a description of Lavinia laid out for the mourners: "Someone, Louisa, of course, Asa told himself had arranged her hair softly, and folded her hands over the Prayer Book bound in white velvet, she had carried at her wedding." It may have occurred to Ellen Glasgow that Lavinia's friends probably would not have gone so far in their preparations or that the Prayer Book was too blatant an irony to introduce at this serious moment.

Readers of A Certain Measure know how important Ellen Glasgow considered point of view in her novels.[21] Although it is an element of her work that at least one important critic has

[21] See especially pages 154 and 180.

strongly condemned,[22] it is clear from the manuscripts of *Beyond Defeat* that she was constantly attentive to it during the composition. Numerous revisions, mostly from the second draft on, show her very much concerned to center the point of view on Roy, whom she had selected very early as the center of consciousness. In spite of this there are lapses (whether intentional or not we cannot tell) even in the final state of the text. Parts of the opening episode shift the point of view to the old aunt, and one whole chapter, where Craig and Kate speak with Roy off the scene, shifts it away from Roy entirely. The point of view also shifts back and forth rather freely between Asa and Roy throughout the whole of the last part of the book. Yet if there is no strict maintenance of the point of view, the novelette can hardly be said to suffer because of it.

The revision of point of view includes the addition of such phrases as "she said to herself" or "she thought" to make it clear that what follows is not asserted by the author, but is Roy's own thought. These revisions also include a few places where the point of view is simply shifted from another character to Roy. Consider, for example, this passage in the first draft: "Watching Roy's face with the drawn features and the deep gaze she thought vaguely "How changed she is! How utterly changed! Yet how extraordinarily alive!" Here, Charlotte is thinking to herself. But because this violates the centering on Roy's consciousness the passage was changed in the second draft to: "Her eyes, perplexed and hurt, were on Roy's face and the girl could feel her thoughts as if they were spoken aloud! How changed she is! How utterly changed!"

A number of revisions related to point of view concern this question of whether the character or the author herself is thinking or feeling something. These changes do not follow a dis-

[22] Frederick Hoffman, *The Modern Novel in America* (Chicago: Henry Regnery Co., 1951), pp. 65–75.

tinct pattern. For instance, the phrase "my memory too faint" is revised to "her memory too faint." The question here is why Roy should stop speaking and Ellen Glasgow start. No single reason could explain each of these instances. Most of the changes in point of view, however, benefit the coherence of the narrative.

Many of the revisions made throughout the composition of *Beyond Defeat* can best be described simply as changes in diction. Changes of a single word, or perhaps of a short phrase, made for any number of particular purposes but usually for the general effect of making the language more precise, catch just the right shade of feeling and thought. The importance to Ellen Glasgow of this part of her craft is apparent in her own discussion of these problems in *A Certain Measure*.[23]

All the drafts of *Beyond Defeat* show the author constantly at work to select *le mot juste*, in the pursuit of which, by her own testimony, she often "searched for hours." Even so late as the last draft there are many instances of words being changed to create a slight modification in tone. The earlier drafts are extremely difficult to read in places because of the number of substitutions tried before the author hit on the right word.

A number of other revisions in diction were obviously made to avoid inappropriate—sometimes ludicrous—connotations. In the first draft Kate Oliver is said to be strong as an "ox," but this was later revised to "oak," to avoid the decidedly unfeminine connotations of the earlier word. In the same way, when Craig kisses Roy he is said to kiss her "rapidly," but this was altered to "roughly."

Many of the changes in diction appear to have been made to catch the American idiom better. Words or phrases with a slight ring of Anglicism to them were usually revised. The nurse, for example, speaks of getting a "place," but this was

[23] See especially pages 205–6.

changed later to "job." Elsewhere "pierced her through" was revised to "pierced through her"; "of a sudden" became "suddenly"; and "but for" was altered to "if it wasn't for." Curiously, however, some of these revisions work in the opposite direction. "Eat your lunch" became "Make a good lunch," and "You made a mess of things" was changed to "You made a muddle of things." In other instances, "nearest chair" was dropped for "chair nearest" and "Has he been missing long?" became "Has he been long missing?"

The somewhat more formal tone of *Beyond Defeat* as compared with that of *In This Our Life* comes in large part from the simplicity of the language of the sequel, particularly the dialogue, and from a conscious attempt to change the fast, clipped style of *In This Our Life* to a mellower, slower moving language. A number of revisions exemplify the new direction in style toward plainness and an almost Biblical simplicity. Superfluous words in certain phrases are removed so that loose, informal discourse is tightened and made more restrained and formal. For example, "bad" is deleted from "bad heart attack," "almost" from "were almost empty," "good" from "good day nursery," "all" from "But it is all over," and "enough" from "room enough for us all." There are over twenty-five such changes, mostly in the first and second drafts. Yet even in the final draft, Ellen Glasgow made a few more changes of this sort. In this draft, for example, she deleted "comfortably" from "enough to live on comfortably" and "forever" from "before he went out of life forever."

Another attempt to tighten the style of the work and to simplify the flow of the language can be seen in the many revisions which involved only the deletion of commas around adverbial phrases. These might be viewed simply as Ellen Glasgow's recognition of the tendency in modern writing toward lighter internal punctuation in sentences, but I feel it also reflects her awareness of the movement of her prose because these deletions lessen the somewhat static quality characteristic of her writing as a whole. There are over a hundred such deletions, slightly more of them in the first than in the second half of the text. A typical example occurs in the third draft. The commas she deleted there are enclosed in brackets: "Yes, I suppose so," Charlotte began[,] vaguely, and[,] collecting her faculties, added[,] with firm assurance, "Why, of course she is still your mother." Even with these deletions, there is still a marked tendency for some sentences to become static under the weight of heavy internal punctuation. Consider, for example, the following, which was left to stand in the final version of the text: "She shuffled, rheumatically, out of the room, while Roy listened, with suspended breath, for the sound of a ponderous tread on the stairs."

One final kind of minor revision in the third draft is of interest in the matter of style. That is the change to English rather than American spellings of certain words. Thus, "color" is revised to "colour" in three places, though, probably inadvertently, it is left standing in one other. Ellen Glasgow's reason for preferring English spellings has never been clear, but the fact that in at least four cases she put down the American spelling first seems to indicate the preference was not altogether a matter of habit.

Ellen Glasgow was well aware that part and chapter divisions can indicate to the reader certain qualities of the narrative, and accordingly we find revisions in these divisions between the first and second drafts. Most significant is the addition in the second draft of the roman numeral indicating the third chapter of Part One. This necessitated, of course, changing the numbers of all the subsequent chapters of Part One in the second draft. The reason for the addition seems to have been that the narrative shifts rather abruptly at this point from Roy's past to

Asa's present. To someone reading through the book for the first time, the reason might not be readily apparent because the characters "on stage" remain the same and no significant turn in the action has taken place at the end of the second chapter. Like this revision, the expansion between the first and second drafts of the names of the parts of the novelette, from "Morning" to "Morning: The Shadow," from "Afternoon" to "Afternoon: The Substance," and from "Evening" to "Evening: The Light in the Sky," is a significant and functional revision that clearly aids the reader's understanding of some of the book's symbolism and augments the sense of the compactness of the narrative by indicating the short time span of the action.

The change of the subtitle in the second draft from "Epilogue to a Life" to "Epilogue to an Era" is also of interest. "Life" may have referred to Lavinia, Charlotte, and Asa's generation, but it may have referred simply to Lavinia and her death at the end of *Beyond Defeat*. The change to "Era" seems wise because it indicates that not just the people of one generation were being replaced or were passing away at the beginning of World War II, but that an era, the cultural and moral background of a span of history, had ended.

## IV

If I am correct in assuming that the methods of composing and revising *Beyond Defeat* are truly representative of those employed from *Barren Ground* on, then the manuscript material associated with *Beyond Defeat* grants valuable insight into Ellen Glasgow's working methods in her major phase. What these manuscripts offer partly explains, partly corroborates, and partly calls into question what the author herself had said in works she published on her craft and consequently they serve to clarify the nature of her fiction, both as she understood it and as it actually is.

The manuscripts show, first of all, a conscientious craftsman; that is, a writer who relied not on intuitive faculties, but on conscious, systematic methods for composing and revising a work. Even in the first draft, her writing is not a spontaneous outpouring or a product of infallible intuition, but a conscious attempt to keep the various elements of fiction—action and plot, characterization, theme, and atmosphere—in controlled balance. And the succeeding drafts show still further attempts at the proper coordination of these elements in a generally systematic way.

The attention to style in the first draft and, indeed, even in some of the notes for the work gives strong evidence that Ellen Glasgow's own account of her concept of style as an organic part of her writing is valid. The concern for closeness to reality and for verisimilitude, revealed both in the rough notes and in the successive drafts of the novelette, supports her concept of herself as essentially a realist and a "social historian of Virginia." Finally, in her concern with the explicit statement of the theme and the relation of the theme to characterization and plot and action we can see Ellen Glasgow's urge to have her ideas understood and something of what she meant when she contended that "the whole truth must embrace the interior world as well as external appearances" and that the purpose of fiction is to convey ideas, as well as feeling and vital experience.[24]

One of the most interesting revelations these manuscripts afford is how Ellen Glasgow went about making *Beyond Defeat* take on a particular flavor and character all its own, even though it had been intended as a sequel to another work. Some of her changes, such as the muting of the undercurrents of

[24] *A Certain Measure*, pp. 260–61.

irony in the characterizations of Asa and Roy, may have removed a measure of vitality from the story, but these changes
serve a larger function well. The means by which these changes
were accomplished show Ellen Glasgow in command of her
style, creating a flexible prose fully capable of serving the ends
she had elected for it in a particular work, with a particular set
of circumstances and a special function in view.

## A NOTE ON THE TEXT

THE text of this edition is from Ellen Glasgow's third draft of
the novelette, and, as it incorporates all the various revisions
she made to that draft, probably represents the latest stage to
which the work had progressed. A cover sheet that includes Mr.
Frank Morley's address at Harcourt, Brace and Company, and
the author's revisions in ink of certain parts as suggested by
Morley, establish this third draft as the one Ellen Glasgow sent
to Morley. It is the manuscript from which the work was to be
printed until plans to publish it were abandoned.

Apparently Morley and other people who read the manuscript made no attempt to correct its numerous typographical
errors. Nor did they change English to American spelling or
delete hyphens from many compound words where they are
ordinarily not used in modern American spelling. These
changes would undoubtedly have been made before publication
to conform the styling of the manuscript to that of *In This Our
Life*. I have corrected the typographical errors, but I have kept
the English spellings and the hyphenations. In the one instance
where "color" appeared, I changed that spelling to conform to
the rest of the manuscript.

Ellen Glasgow used periods in a number of different combi-
nations to indicate ellipses and suspensions of thought, but

three periods, even at the end of a sentence, were the most common, and as that is the way they appear in *In This Our Life,* I have followed that practice throughout.

The present edition, then, conveys accurately the latest stage in the evolution of the book but avoids the encumbrance to the reader of obvious typographical errors and inconsistencies.

# BEYOND DEFEAT
*An Epilogue to an Era*

# PART ONE
## Morning: The Shadow

# I

D o we always return to the place where we have suffered most?

Before she had grasped its meaning, the
thought wavered and slipped from Roy's mind.
She had come back to face life, and life had not waited. Of the
past, nothing was left but herself and the things she remembered. Nothing was here to live down, not even the bare outline
of her old failure. Had the years merely drifted, as dust drifts
without settling, over the house and the street? Yet in those
three vital years, torn up from the deepest roots of her heart,
she had lived and died, and been born over again . . .

There was a brittle edge to the late October sunlight. On the
pavement the shadows of trees looked as if they were carved
out of substance. A sense of dawn was still lingering, she felt, at
the street's sudden end, where the house with dark blinds
appeared more secretive than empty. From the narrow front,
through changing leaves, the sun struck back, slantwise, toward
the thin, pale sky.

The child in Roy's arms struggled to be put down, and she
lowered him to the brick pavement. His weight, light as it was,
had dragged on her strength, which she had never recovered
after a second attack of pneumonia. If I could have kept well,
she said to herself. If only I could have kept well, I need not
have come back . . .

"Birdie!" the child shouted joyously, grasping the air. "Mine!
Birdie!"

"No, darling. We left our birds in New York." Her smile,
which she tried to make bright and natural, creased the faintly

drawn skin round her eyes and mouth. Smiling hurts, she said to herself, and smiled again with a flash of her old gallantry.

"Birdie! Mine!" cried the child, tripping on his short legs after a pigeon, which fluttered up and sank down a little farther away.

In his pointed blue cap with a tassel and his knitted blue suit, which matched his eyes, he looked absurd and adorable, Roy thought, like a child in a fairy-tale. He is all mine, she told herself, while her heart seemed to melt with pity and tenderness. No one else has a share in him, not any one else in the world. Ecstasy, as sharp as anguish, pierced through her, that utterly illogical bliss of being alive, of the recovered fullness of life. Always, with this sensation, she felt a startled thrill of surprise. Was she really awake at last? Could she feel, once more, the old delight in identity, in that lost miracle within, as of a bell ringing: I feel. I know. I am. After the long illness, the poverty, the hunger, after those days and nights in the friendless ward of a strange hospital, after all the failure and the defeat, was there still another world waiting ahead? Resurrection of the body, the doctor had called her awakening, the return of the flesh to life. To return that way, he had said, one must go to the end of heartbreak and come back in a circle . . .

She crossed the pavement, with the child trotting in small, quick steps by her side. Standing before the door, she thought: They will not want me back when they know. Then, as her hand touched the bell: Oh, but there is no other way left to me!

Of a sudden, the door opened, as if someone had waited there through the years. After a moment of dazed bewilderment, while her glance wavered between light and darkness, she distinguished the shapeless bulk of her great-aunt, Mrs.

Fitzroy, grown more placid, more enormous in size, more waxen in colour.

"Don't you know me, Aunt Charlotte?" Shutting the door behind her, Roy lifted her face to be kissed.

For a mute instant, Charlotte peered at her with blinking near-sighted eyes. Then, finding an uncertain voice, she asked: "Is it really you, Roy? Why didn't you write to us?"

"I couldn't. There wasn't anything I could say. Where is Father?" Was it merely a feeling, the girl wondered, or was she pushing her way into the house, while the older woman retreated, step by step, through the hall to the living-room, where the dark blinds were drawn against daylight? Yet nothing was changed, though everything, even the once gay chintz covers Roy had made, appeared faded and drab. "Where is Father?" she repeated.

Mrs. Fitzroy shook her head with a negative gesture, which rippled down through her solid mass, and settled her finally between the wings of the chair nearest. "I spent the night here," she said, as if Roy had not spoken. "Your mother was threatened with a heart attack, and she wanted one of the family beside her. Andrew is in the Navy, and Maggie has no nurse for the new baby. Would you mind letting in some light?"

After raising the shades, Roy turned round to face her. "Where is Father? Where is . . ."

"I was just going." Charlotte babbled on before Roy had finished her question. "Your mother is better, and the doctor thinks there is no danger. I like to do my marketing early. The war has made everything so scarce." Without a perceptible change of mood, she inquired blandly, "Why didn't you write to me after your Uncle William died?"

"I couldn't." Roy was gasping. "Oh, I couldn't! You don't

know . . ." Then, more urgently, "Where is Father, Aunt Charlotte?"

Reluctantly, Mrs. Fitzroy's eyes came to rest on the girl's arm encircling the child. "Whose child is that, Roy?" she broke in, without answering.

"Mine." Roy's tone was unfaltering, but she shivered slightly, as if an inner chill ran through her nerves. "He is mine, Aunt Charlotte."

"You might have written us that you were married again. It has been more than three years, and in all that time you wrote only once. Or was it twice? We wondered whether you had died up there, and nobody had taken the trouble to let us know."

Roy shook her head. "No, I did not die. I was ill, but I never wanted to die, not even when . . . when . . ." Her knees gave way and she dropped on a sofa, drawing the child with her. "But I wasn't married," she said firmly.

"You don't mean? Oh, Roy you can't mean . . ." Though she had intended to hasten out to her marketing, Mrs. Fitzroy sank deeper between the sheltering wings of the chair. Her voice, when she spoke after a panting silence, was barely more than a mutter. "Then that was the reason?"

"Yes, that was the reason."

"But why? Why?" Charlotte's eyes were bulging with disbelief. "How could such a thing happen to a girl of good family? William was right when he said no girl could be trusted alone in New York."

"It was here. Not in New York." Though Roy's voice broke once from weakness, it was a level break, without vehemence. Regret was lost in a brave acceptance of the past, which was now over, which was obliterated and ended forever. "It was the night I left Craig and ran out into the storm. I thought he had turned back to Stanley. I hated him. I hated them both. I wanted to break something. I wanted to smash up everything I had ever believed in. I wanted to hurt all I cared for . . . Oh, but what is the use? You could never understand, Aunt Charlotte, you could never . . ."

Charlotte's eyes had closed, and her heavy head nodded, as if she were in a trance or asleep. "No, I cannot understand," she mumbled while Roy was still talking. "I cannot believe it."

"I hate to hurt you," Roy said. "I hated to come home."

Charlotte's sagging figure jerked upright, as if a steel rod had shot through her spine, and her startled eyes popped open. "But where else could you have gone," she asked, "except to your family? That's a bad cough," she added gently, "and you look," her lips tightened over the word, "starved."

"There is something wrong with my lungs. It began with pneumonia. I had pneumonia twice. The doctor said I couldn't live unless I gave up work and went away to be cured. But that would take six months, and there wasn't anybody, not anybody in the world, I could leave my child with. I thought Father would look after him."

"Wait a minute. I'll give you an egg with some brandy. There isn't anything else in the house. I hope you had a good breakfast."

Roy laughed. "A cup of coffee at the station. That and Timothy's orange juice and cereal took my last penny. I had saved the fare for the bus, but I left my suitcase at the station."

"I will see what I can find. There was trouble with the cook last night, and she left without giving notice. That brought on your mother's heart attack. What with the war and relief, it is hard enough to keep servants at any price, but your mother still refuses to pay higher wages. You remember what extravagant ideas she used to have? Well, since your Uncle William left her enough to live on, she has grown as near as the bark on a tree. Though she has been so ill all summer, she insists on having undergraduate nurses. But for me and for Louisa Littlepage, who drops in every morning, there wouldn't be anybody to look after her. Since the war began," she concluded, with a flash of her old insight, "people take so much less interest in sickness."

"Then Virgie isn't here any longer?"

"Virgie has been doing defense work, and doing it badly, I don't doubt, for the highest wages."

Roy sighed. "I know we used to be poor, but I imagined we were better off nowadays."

Charlotte was on her way to the door, and her answer floated back over her plump shoulder. "You wouldn't notice the change, not with the tight fist your mother keeps on her money."

As Roy patted the rebellious child, she thought vaguely: Why did I come home? Couldn't I have found some better place? Aloud, she said, "Oh, hush, Timothy. You must be good now, my darling."

She was murmuring over the words, when Charlotte waddled in, with a glass in her hand. "We made eggnog for your mother last night, and the nurse left the bottle out of the sideboard. That," she added, while she watched Roy gratefully sipping, "was what started the trouble. The cook left with a full basket, after giving us a great deal of impudence, and the shelves were empty this morning. But I found these two eggs hidden away. They ought to stay you till lunch time. We are having it early."

"Then you haven't had breakfast."

"Oh, the day nurse scraped up something when she came on duty. Now, I am going out to bring in our lunch. Is there any special diet for the little boy?"

"Don't bother about us, Aunt Charlotte. We can eat anything, and we're always hungry. Timothy has never been coddled."

"Timothy?" Charlotte repeated the name, in a tone that sounded as if she were discreetly edging away. "I never heard that name on either side of the family."

Roy nodded. "Yes, I know. It did not mean anything, and I liked it."

Charlotte had picked up her bag, and was rummaging in its bottom for her market-list. Then, having sorted out the list, she turned and glanced back, with an avid gleam of curiosity. "The more I think of you, Roy, the less I can understand . . ."

"I did not care what happened to me," Roy answered, as if she were reciting a speech she had learned by heart, and then almost forgotten. "I suppose it was madness . . . But you've never known madness."

"I think," Charlotte remarked, grasping after the suavity that was slipping away. "I think every one of us must have known madness, at least once in a lifetime."

"That's only in looking back. At the time I couldn't see. I didn't know. All I wished to do was to separate myself from the rest of you. Yes, from you, too, and even from Father. I wanted to hurt whatever it was that had hurt me, that had made me trust in things that were not true, that had never been true . . . But, of course," her voice dropped, "I made a worse muddle of everything. In the end I had to come home."

Charlotte groaned, but, since she was gifted with a humane nature, she probed tenderly. "Even then, Roy, I cannot see. I cannot see how you brought yourself to . . . to . . ."

"Oh, that" . . . Roy looked down on the child's head in her lap. "That wasn't desperation . . . at least not entirely . . ."

"Then what? What?" Charlotte snapped the words in two before Roy had found the one that she needed.

"I'm trying to tell you. If you will give me time, Aunt Charlotte, I am trying to tell you. You used to be so patient, and now, now . . ."

"There was never anything like this. We never had anything like this in . . . in our family . . ."

"I am trying to tell you." Roy repeated the phrase because it was the only one in her mind. "I am trying to tell you that I found someone who was more unhappy than I was . . ."

"But you couldn't have cared for him. There was Craig. And you were wrong about Craig, Roy. Your besetting sin was always impatience. But, even then, how could it have happened?"

"I don't know how or why, but it did happen, Aunt Charlotte. I am trying to tell you," she hesitated, broke down, and began again. "He needed love more . . . more than . . ."

"How long had you known him?"

"Only for that one night in the storm. He was trying to lose himself just as I was. We had both wandered for hours. He found me in a little pavilion, where a band used to play in summer. It was over on the other side of the city, in the old part of Queenborough. I was wet through, and it had turned suddenly chill . . . He was as young as I, and I could see that he was lost and unhappy. He was good, too. I knew he was good, and it was not fair that he should be so wretched . . . But he would always, I knew, be on the outside. He would not ever, so long as he lived, be a part of life." She bit back her words sharply, and then stumbled on. "That was more than three years ago. It was the end of that August, when Stanley was upsetting things, because Peter was dead, and she wanted Craig back again . . ."

"I know, I know," Charlotte groaned. "It all hastened your Uncle William's death."

"Well, that was the man," Roy said quietly. "He was going

to sail by the next boat for England. He knew, or felt, that war was beginning, and he wanted to lose himself in the war because he would not feel that he was alone. There was a horrible scar on his face. Otherwise, he was . . . oh, well, I suppose you would call him good-looking. I felt sorry for him. I felt sorrier than I have ever felt for anyone else in the world. He was so dreadfully apart and alone. I wanted to make up, in some way, for what he missed. I wanted to give him a little happiness before . . . before he went out of life. And now," she finished in her steady voice, "I suppose he is dead . . . or . . . or worse off. Sometimes I think of him in the night."

"But, still," Charlotte muttered, "I do not see why you could let yourself. After all, what do you know of him?" Her eyes, perplexed and hurt, were on Roy's face, and the girl could feel her thoughts as if they were spoken aloud: How changed she is! How utterly changed!

"I know," Roy was saying, "that he was born in Canterbury, and that he was more unhappy than I was."

"And that is all?"

"That is all."

"But his name? You have not told me his name."

"I never knew his name. It was all over. I knew what I had done, and I wanted never to see him again. As soon as I went out into the street," she was making a fruitless effort to be understood, "I came to myself. Nothing mattered any longer, not even about Craig and Stanley. Somehow, I don't know how it was, pity did not seem to wear any better than . . . than anger . . . I meant to put it all out of my life. I expected to get a job in New York, and never come back. But, you see, I did not know then about Timothy."

Charlotte sighed. She must have forgotten her new apartment, which she loved, and her early marketing, which Roy knew she enjoyed. She appeared to have forgotten, too, that

Roy was hungry and had had no breakfast. "That is the kind of thing," she said, with the stern platitude of the traditional mind, "that is not possible—with people like us."

"Anything is possible with any kind of people."

A moaning sound broke from Charlotte's lips. "How did you live, Roy?"

"At first I got a job. That wasn't so hard till I had to give up and go to the hospital. I was never really well after that. They said I ought to have rested longer, but everything cost so much that I . . . well, I lived very close, and I did not always have the right kind of food. While I was working, too, I had to put Timothy in a day nursery, and that was expensive. But he was well cared for. Doesn't he look well cared for?"

Charlotte assented indifferently. "He is a handsome child. But what," she demanded, with severity, "can a child like that expect from the future?"

"At first, I thought I couldn't go through with it." Roy's voice had hardened. "But I did in the end, and afterwards I was thankful. I wouldn't give him up, not now, for everything else in the world."

"You always liked children. I remember you wanted a child when you were married to Peter. It was Peter who said you could not afford it. After Peter died, I thought . . . oh, well, I thought . . ." Her tongue more than her mind seemed to stumble and trip over the words. "If only . . . if only he were Peter's son . . ."

Roy gazed at her steadily. "That would not make any difference. Sometimes I feel that I love him better because so much is unknown, and cannot ever be known. He is not only my child, but he is part of the future. That gives him a kind of mystery. There was mystery in Peter . . ."

"Peter broke your heart," Charlotte answered, in her quaint Victorian idiom. "But, after Peter, you loved Craig, and I hoped you would be happy. The fault was that you could not trust life. You could never really trust Craig."

"I trusted Peter. That taught me," Roy answered, with bitterness.

Charlotte moved uneasily. "What were you called in New York? Did you keep Peter's name?"

"They called me Lavinia Roy. I took my old name—only I left off the Fitzroy, because of Mother. I knew she would not like that. Many women in New York keep their own names."

"I know, and I remember how, as a child, you disliked being called Little Lavinia." Charlotte was gazing at the ring on Roy's hand. "It must have been hard for you."

"They did not know I had ever been married till . . . till Timothy was coming. Then I had to say something. I told them," her tone was deeply cadenced, "that Timothy's father was in the army . . . the British Army. Afterwards, I let them think he had been killed." Her face went suddenly blank. "I have told you everything, Aunt Charlotte. Isn't everything enough for you?"

The child was sleeping, sprawled on the short sofa, with his head in Roy's lap. His thick curls, more golden than chestnut, would have made even Stanley's amber hair appear darker.

"He is not like you," Charlotte murmured. "His colouring is different from either the Timberlakes or the Fitzroys." Her forehead puckered, and again Roy could feel the thought under her transparent expression: Though she wished no harm to anyone, her look confessed, not even to the father of Roy's nameless child, she could not deny that his being safely dead would make everything easier. "But what on earth," she jerked her slouching figure erect, "are we to do with this child?"

Shocked, apparently, by the change in Roy's face, Charlotte bent over the girl and smoothed the short waves of hair, which seemed to have lost the old lustre. "You look worn out, Roy.

We have talked too long. Will you come to my apartment? After William died, I sold Fitzroyal, and I moved into an apartment in town. Do you feel faint?" she inquired anxiously.

"No, I'm all right. I'd like to give Timothy a bath and put him to bed. We got so little sleep last night. The noise frightened him." Slipping the child's head from her lap, she helped him to stand on his feet. "Is anybody in my old rooms?"

"No, they are vacant, but I doubt if the beds are made. The nurses dress in Stanley's room next to Lavinia."

Roy shivered. "Stanley is not here then?"

"I thought you knew. You seem not to have heard anything."

"Where is she?"

"In California. Lavinia sent her out there, and she was married within a few weeks. Her husband is quite old, but he is very wealthy. He has something to do with the movies."

Roy gazed at her in surprise. "Oh, but I thought Craig . . ."

"You ran away without thinking. Craig was only sorry for her. Pity seems to have ruined both your worlds."

"I ruined mine." Roy looked years older in an instant. "I ruined everything."

"Well, I must go now. I will bring whatever I can find in market, and we will have an early lunch. Then we must talk it all over, and we can decide what is best to be done. No matter what happens, you ought not to let that cough run on."

Hurrying out on her rheumatic legs, which were willing but weak, Charlotte went through the hall to the front door, while Roy looked, with a puzzled frown, after her swaying figure. "I shall have to stay," she thought. "Whether I live or die, and no matter how much they hate doing it, they will have to keep Timothy." Clutching the child in her arms, she said gaily, "There are lots and lots of pigeons here, darling, and they will love having you."

# II

OTHING here has forgotten, Roy thought. This room is listening for Peter's voice. A door in the present was flung wide, and she was swept into time that was not a dark current, but a still backwater. She had lived here with Peter, and with Peter alone she had lived days and nights of pure ecstasy. But Peter had killed her youth. Life and Peter together had killed her youth and that ecstasy . . .

The room and these inanimate objects had watched both her ecstasy and her anguish. They had watched her casual parting with Peter, when he had left her for Stanley—for Stanley who, but for that sudden madness, would in three days have been married to Craig. In this room, amid these objects, Roy had endured the agony and the despair of injured love, and of tortured pride, which was sharper even than the wounding of love. And after that, long after that, the room had watched the beginning and the end of her love for Craig, who had loved her, in his way, but had turned again, or seemed to turn in pity, to Stanley. For, in her passion and her madness, Stanley had destroyed Peter . . . Well, all that was over, and done with, and cast off by time. Out of the old ecstasy and anguish had come Timothy, and Timothy belonged, not with the buried past, but with that endless becoming which was the unknown, and as yet the unborn, future.

Life defeated me, Roy told herself, and an instant later, with her challenging air: but life does not end with defeat. Except in fable, victory or defeat settles nothing but a single moment in history. In death, and in death alone, is there finality. Life would still go on for the living, and for those who had lost, as well as for those who had won, the old end would fall away, inevitably, from the new beginning . . .

Bathed and dressed, the child lay asleep on one of the twin beds, under a blue blanket Roy had left here, in the hall closet, three years before. Nothing was altered. Even the two pairs of blue blankets, adorned with her monogram, and given to her by Aunt Charlotte, were still soft and downy. In that other life— or was it another eternity?—love was all she had wanted for happiness. First, she had loved Peter, and then, when she lost Peter, she had turned to Craig, seeking only to satisfy some imperative demand in her own nature. But it was neither Peter nor Craig, she saw, in an extraordinary flash of vision, it was love she had needed. What she had craved was the perfection that is in love, even though love itself cannot ever become perfect.

Oh, but now she was safe! Overtaken by the past, she could stand bravely amid the fragments of what she had once thought of as happiness. She had found her heart invulnerable to memory. She had fought on beyond defeat, and she had won the kind of peace that is victory. When I am well again, she told herself, I shall have learned how to make over my life. I shall have learned how to find happiness. Perhaps the past had to be. Perhaps it would have been what it was, whether or not I was a part of it.

A bath had refreshed her, but when she lay down on her old bed, her eyelids jerked open, as if they were moved by wires, and she gazed, not hopelessly, not even unhappily, through the small window, where two white pigeons flashed and twinkled in the glittering air, and a tall church spire was etched against the blue emptiness of the sky. Everything was as she had known it would be, even the shadowy fall of the leaves, even the slow, retarded rhythm of wings in the sunlight. Yes, it was all the same, yet how different!

Aunt Charlotte had called Timothy a handsome child, and he was beautiful. As Roy leaned on her elbow and looked down on him, an irrepressible joy again shone in her eyes. He was lying on his side, with his roseleaf cheek pressed into the pillow and a soft duskiness melting under his long eyelashes. Though she could not remember the colour of his father's eyes, she felt that Timothy's glance, when it darted past her, was as gay as the song of a bluebird. Only the thick, upspringing curls, as they clustered back from his forehead, reminded her of the man she had known for that one stormy evening. Yet the father's hair was darker, with none of the child's brilliant fairness. And I can remember nothing of that evening, she said to herself, except an unhappiness more desperate than mine. All that happened was my fault, not his. It happened, because of my longing to revenge myself on what I had most loved and valued. Yet she had not been revenged. She had hurt nobody but herself, and perhaps Timothy. Yes, she had hurt Timothy most of all, though now, when no choice was left to her, she would give her life to spare him the pain that was ahead in the future. But she was not thinking of Timothy on that night, in that strange room, with the dim glow and the flapping shutter, and outside the rain and wind on the sycamore, while the world beyond was dissolving into water and flowing away. Was she thinking then of hate and of her fruitless revenge on the only life she had known? For the things she had wished to destroy were still here; they were still untouched and untroubled.

I was wrong then, she thought, and perhaps I am wrong now. Yet out of the other wrong Timothy came; and because of Timothy, I found courage, and I found as well, something else that is nearly, if not quite, happiness. Timothy was the last thing I imagined on that night of despair and hatred, and of pity too. But Timothy had given her, not only courage but endurance, and more than this, the purest satisfaction—or was it fulfillment?—that she was ever likely to feel. This, at least, was what the nurse had told her she ought to feel, when, for the first time after his birth, Timothy was brought to be fed from her breast. And this was told her, yet again, by that look of female perfection, of instinctive, unreasoning rapture, on the faces of the other women in the maternity ward. These women, in that special moment, all wore an identical expression she had never seen anywhere else. It was a look that could spring only from some physical essence within, a look so intensely self-absorbed, so self-important even, that she wondered why it did not set up a barrier between them and their husbands, if they had husbands, as some of them, she suspected, had not, and would never have . . .

Well, she for one, and for the only one among them, had felt, in the beginning, no such benediction. Her fulfillment had come later, for, through these earlier months, she had resented the coming of Timothy, though, even then, she had not reached the final desperation in which she could safely do away with him, and deny him, in mercy or in fear, the life she had summoned from chaos. He was conceived in a storm. He had entered a world which was torn, through violence, to fragments. In his small unknown identity he embodied the future. No, it was not mercy, it was not humanity, that refused to destroy him. It was, she saw now, nothing more than the mood of defeat against which she had fought in the long months before he was born. Though it was true, as Aunt Charlotte reminded her, that she had wanted a child, the only child she could have welcomed would have been the child of her happiest years, the child that Peter, young and eager, and poor and craving success, had denied her. Oh, but what nonsense, she said to herself, is talked about motherhood! She had loved Timothy afterwards. She had loved him, because he was dependent upon her, not for life alone, but for happiness and a reason for living. And because, too, he is lovable, and nobody, not even Aunt Charlotte, could help loving him.

If only I had health and a place somewhere, I could make him happy, she told herself, and I could be happy, too, or if not happy, at least contented with life. If I could have that one wish fulfilled, I feel I should never again ask for anything else. But, first of all, before I begin anything, I must go away to be cured . . . How I wish Father would come! She glanced round at her cheap travelling clock, and remembered that, before she went to the hospital, she had sold the wristwatch Uncle William had given to her. It was a good watch, set in a circle of small diamonds, and she wondered who was wearing it now. Uncle William, who used to boast that he carried the world in his pocket, was dead, with all his proud world in ruins . . .

A bell rang somewhere, two flights away, and presently she heard footsteps descending the staircase. The nurse, she supposed, was answering the ring; and a few minutes later, she recognized Mrs. Fitzroy's tread mounting the stairs. A man carrying Roy's suitcase hastened in, mumbled, "The lady paid me," and ran out hurriedly. Aunt Charlotte was coming nearer; she had passed Lavinia's closed door, and slowly, following a long pause, in which she collected her breath, her large, benign yet anxious face, rose, like a troubled moon, over the landing.

"I am not used to stairs now," she said, gasping. "I am thankful I live in an apartment." Thrusting a brown paper bag into Roy's hands, she added, while she fell into the stoutest chair in the room, "We are having lunch so early I did not bring anything but a bun for Timothy."

After a glance at the sleeping child, Roy put aside the unopened bag. "Does Mother know I am here?"

"Yes, the nurse had to tell her. Lavinia heard you walking overhead."

"What will you say? I mean about Timothy?"

"Heaven only knows! It will have to come to me."

"Do you think she will take care of him?"

Charlotte frowned dubiously. "Not if I know her. I think he will deal her the worst blow she has ever had, and it will not be easy for her to forget that. Of course, I may be talking like an old lady . . . but, after all, I am an old lady. I am going on seventy-eight, and Lavinia will never see sixty-five."

"Would she rather I had deserted Timothy?" Roy's face clouded, while her hand hovered over the child's head.

"I imagine she would rather you had both talked and acted like a lady. And surely no lady, old or young, has ever acted after your wild fashion."

"I know," Roy admitted. "But look at Timothy. Who could help loving him?"

An old and tired smile, the smile of secret wisdom, Roy thought, crossed, but did not curve, the soft, straight line of Mrs. Fitzroy's lips. "What was your idea, Roy, in bringing a child without a father to a place like Queenborough?"

"Oh, but I told you, Aunt Charlotte. You said it was the only thing I could do." Her cough choked her. "If I am not cured . . . If I die, and Timothy had been left in New York, he would be put in some institution. I've been driven almost mad by that fear. It would have happened to him if I had not lived through pneumonia."

"I see," Charlotte lingered over the syllable. "You do look as if you had gone hungry," she continued, with a natural sympathy for the undernourished. "Do you mean that you actually went without having enough to eat?"

Roy frowned impatiently. "Oh, there were lean days in between jobs. It was harder to find work after I came out of the hospital. If only I could tell you what I learned about hospitals! But nobody wanted to employ a girl who had been ill, and could not afford to wear the right clothes or to buy the right lipstick. My last work was in a department store, and I was so shabby they put me down in the basement. Then the bad air made me cough so much I lost my job. But I am not worrying about that . . . I am simply obliged to get well again, because I can't leave Timothy as long as he needs me."

"I see," Charlotte repeated.

"She is still my mother," Roy said.

"Yes, I suppose so," Charlotte began vaguely, and collecting her faculties, added with firm reassurance, "Why, of course she is still your mother."

Roy looked at her with a disconsolate smile. "If only she will not talk about sin."

"Well, you will have to listen. All the Fitzroys thought too much about sin, even poor William. He grew up in the Reconstruction period, you know, and he had so few other pleasures." She sighed, and continued, in a mildly reflective mood: "Not that sin ever meant much to me. My temptation, Craig used to tell me, was toward genteel behaviour." Stopping abruptly, she screwed up her near-sighted eyes and searched Roy's features with a bewildered gaze. "I don't like your shocking thinness, and the loss of your fresh complexion. Your colour is bright enough, but it isn't the colour of health."

"I know." Roy's tone held no trace of self-pity. "I have gone off terribly, Aunt Charlotte."

"Well, you will soon pick up. All your face needs is to fill out a bit. And you look, somehow, as if you had fought hard and won a kind of peace . . . or, it may be only the courage to keep up. You have lost that restless look. I noticed the same thing in your father, the one time I have seen him since . . ." Overcome by confusion, she turned away and tried to swallow her words. "I mean . . . I mean . . ."

"I did come through, Aunt Charlotte. And there is a sort of comfort in feeling you can't, ever again, go through the worst . . I used to be afraid of so many things . . . of losing Peter . . that Peter might stop loving me. Then, with Craig and

Stanley, all over and over . . . As long as you love that way, wanting to hold on, you are obliged to live with fear in your mind, and living with fear is the worst that can happen . . . Then I lost Peter, and afterwards I lost Craig, or thought I had lost him; but I found that still I could come through and go on, and even make something of the life I had left. That was why having Timothy was different . . . I mean, when I learned to think just what I could give him to make up, and never, not ever for a single minute, let myself look back on the worst part of it, on all the fear that went on, day after day, month after month . . . As soon as I am cured, we are going to be happy, Timothy and I, and he is going to have a splendid life in spite . . . oh, in spite of everything that is behind us . . ."

"You were always brave, Roy, even if you were reckless. It takes character to build a life on mistakes; and, after all, I suppose, character is an end itself. Anyhow, we believed that in my generation."

But Roy was grazing into the mirror over her dressing table, as if she expected to find an answer in her slightly blurred image. More than three years had passed since she had looked into this mirror, through the pale band of sunshine, which filtered in under the changing leaves. The mirror was still the same, and so was the autumn sunshine, and so were the autumn leaves. The only thing that had altered was the face in the glass. "I look ten years older," she said aloud. "I am only twenty-six, and I might be any age." Her words trailed off into a small wistful laugh. "Do you see the lines round my eyes, and round my mouth . . . Well, that's what having character does for you." Gray eyes under dark surprised eyebrows laughed back at her. The delicate contour of her features had not coarsened, nor had her short, blunt nose, nor her gallant smile etched in with a bright derision. But the struggle had left a constant shadow under the brightness.

"Something must be arranged," Charlotte said. "Do you know where you can go?"

"There is a place in the Adirondacks. The doctor at the hospital has something to do with it, and he can send me there as a patient. They let you stay six months or a year, for almost nothing. It is run for people like me. Only they never take children."

"You couldn't expect it. Not with sick people." Charlotte glanced nervously at the child. "But something can be arranged," she repeated.

"I will talk to Father," Roy said, "when he comes home this evening. Even if Mother doesn't want Timothy, Father will keep him."

"You must not count on that, Roy. He is not coming." Charlotte's tired voice quavered and sank, and picked up a reedy note. "You will have to know, sooner or later. Your mother feels bitterly. I suppose I can't blame her."

Roy's face blanched to a lifeless pallor. "Oh, but Father! Are you trying to tell me Father is dead?" She broke down, while a spasm of pain shuddered through her. "Not Father!" she cried out. "I thought I could bear anything . . . but not Father!"

"No . . . no. Stop, Roy. Nothing has happened . . . at least nothing like that . . . I saw him only a few months ago. He looked well, and he looked happy. I think he is as happy as he can be in a world at war, when he does not know where you are . . . nor whether you are living or dead."

Roy's hands dropped to her lap, and she raised her eyes, which were still brimming with tears. "Then I may see him . . . but you said . . . Oh, you said . . ."

# III

OVERWHELMED by the girl's distress, Charlotte felt that her inelastic arteries were drumming. "You can't see him, Roy. He isn't here. He never comes to the house. Lavinia feels bitterly . . . For myself, I don't know . . . I was always very fond of Asa. I think there is a great deal to be said on his side. And after you left him, and never sent him so much as a word . . ." Out of breath and panting heavily, Charlotte could only press her large, smooth, milk-white hand to her heaving bosom.

"But why has he gone? And where is he? Oh, try to tell me, Aunt Charlotte. I must know. I can't bear not to know."

"I am trying," Charlotte moaned. "I am trying to get my breath. It was after he lost his place in the factory. That was before we went into the war. They were turning off most of the older men . . . and anyone could see that your father was breaking up. He was over sixty, and he'd never had a day's holiday in his life that I could remember. But, I think, most of all," she concluded reproachfully, "it was not hearing from you. It was the way you ran off and left him . . ."

"I know," Roy sobbed. "I'll never, never forgive myself."

"Then . . . well, he had nothing to do, and things seemed to be getting worse with your mother. I can't say I blame him. He'd had a mean life, though, of course, I wish he had not gone down to Kate Oliver's place."

"You mean . . . ?"

"I'm not hinting at anything. Some people think so, but others say they are too old for a scandal. She must be at least fifty-five. Anyhow, they are down there together. The old overseer died at Hunter's Fare, and you know how Asa always was

26

about life on a farm, with a pack of dogs at his heels. That was one of the troubles he had in his marriage. Lavinia made him give up his dogs."

"You mean he has really left Mother?"

"If you like to put it that way. All I mean is that he's taken the overseer's place at Hunter's Fare, and looks happier than I ever imagined he could."

Roy frowned. "I suppose people are talking. Mother must hate that."

"They aren't talking so much as you might think. What with the war and the servant problem, and . . . well, everything else, appearances do not mean what they meant, even three years ago. Still, it wouldn't be natural for Lavinia not to be hurt."

"Doesn't she see him?"

"She refuses to let him come to the house. That, of course, makes it look worse. Nobody knows what the situation is; but he is helping to raise food for the Government, and that is a kind of excuse. There wasn't any other work so important for a man of his age."

The child stirred on the bed, and Roy, turning quickly, bent over him. For an instant, it seemed to Charlotte, the girl's whole being was absorbed in her son, and every other thought, even concern for her father, was swept out of her mind. Not until Timothy was again resting quietly did she glance round at her aunt. "He is upset after the trip," she said. "He had never been on a train before." Then, picking up the thread she had dropped, she continued, as if she were animated by only half of her consciousness, while Charlotte thought, with mild exasperation: I suppose it's because I've never had a child that mothers seem to me so unnatural.

"Father never had any sort of life," Roy was saying, "but I didn't dream he felt it so much."

"None of us imagined it. That's why people won't believe

there's anything in it. Everybody knows that Kate Oliver is one of the best women on earth. And Asa," she insisted bluntly, "is a good man. It makes me feel, somehow—I don't know how—that you can't judge people by the way they act."

"I always knew Father was too good for us. I suppose that was why we did not consider him more." Roy swallowed a sob, and went on in a shaking voice. "If he were here, I'd feel safe about Timothy."

"Well, he isn't here, and you will have to manage without him. You will have to choose between him and your mother."

"Do you mean I can't see him? Not ever . . . ?"

"Not while you are here. Not while you leave your child with Lavinia."

"But will she keep Timothy?"

"I don't know, Roy. All I can say is, I don't know. I can't see what she would do with him."

"It won't be for long. I'll get well as quick as I can. I am obliged to get well." She stretched out appealing hands. "Couldn't you keep him for me, Aunt Charlotte?"

Looking at Roy's pathetic hands, veined with blue under skin the colour of parchment, Charlotte reflected, in the form of a prayer: I am thankful, O Lord, that I was never a mother! From the ample freedom of widowhood, she gazed, with remote pity, upon the girl who had been a childless wife, and was now a mother and widowed, without those compensations that have been well-earned by marriage. Heaven alone knew what Charlotte's marriage, lasting over fifty years, had cost her in fortitude; and she was determined not to surrender the belated rewards of that long sacrifice. At last, in the brief time ahead of her, she was at liberty to consult her own mind, her own inclinations. She thought of her cheerful and wholly modern apartment, designed and furnished, to the most trivial detail, with an eye for the sober comforts of the bereaved. She thought of congenial gatherings, in St. Augustine during the winter season, with other elderly and hopeless widows, and with widowers who were even more elderly, but still hopeful. She thought of enjoyable hours of gossip and of war knitting, on the shaded verandahs of the best summer hotels. Eagerly, she thought, too, of bridge parties, and of enthralled days and nights at the romantic motion pictures she loved, without William, but with a companion of her own choosing. No . . . Oh, no . . . She told herself firmly. I have spent all my life doing what William wished, and one whole lifetime of that has been more than enough for me . . .

"Not at my age," she said aloud. "At my age it is too much to ask of me. Why, I never even wanted a child of my own. The trouble with you young people," she continued, on a note of moral indignation, "is that you take your pleasure, and then try to let somebody else shoulder your responsibility. I will do what I can to help you, Roy, but I cannot, in my old age, be expected to upset my life. If you had shown a little reason, none of this need have happened. You spoiled your own life, and you spoiled Craig's life, and I am not at all sure that you did not drive Asa away from his family . . . you and Stanley between you."

"I know." Roy's voice was trembling, but she met Charlotte's rebuke with defenseless understanding. "I failed everybody. But, after all, failure isn't the end of things. You have to go on, somehow, somewhere. I made a muddle of my life, but here I am, still in the midst of it, and I can't get away." She laughed with a faint echo of gay derision. "But I don't want to die. I like the taste of living. I like the feel of it. I haven't finished with happiness. Why, I haven't even begun yet." Her eyes were luminous with expectancy. Or was this transparent ardour, Charlotte asked herself, merely the hectic flush of that strange malady?

"Well, you'd better begin with a little nourishment," Charlotte replied, sensibly, while she heaved her bulging figure up from the cushions. "All I know about happiness is that it does not thrive on malnutrition. I hear the nurse going downstairs to prepare lunch. She said she would broil some lamb chops for you, unless you would rather come home with me and bring the child with you."

"You're good, Aunt Charlotte, but I'd rather just stay here. Is there something for Timothy?"

"I brought eggs and oranges and plenty of milk. Then there are the chops and some ground-up steak too. Does he eat meat?"

"Oh, yes, and he is always hungry. You wouldn't know from his shyness with strangers how bright he is, really. He is beginning, too, to pick up any words he hears and string them together, with or without meaning. The only trouble I ever had with him was to break him from crawling after he learned to walk."

"Well, well," Charlotte broke in, with uninterested amiability. "I suppose I'd better speak to your mother while the nurse is out of the room. Don't come downstairs till I call you."

"Shall I bring Timothy?"

Charlotte pursed her lips in perplexity. "You may bring him, unless I tell you not to. After all, she will have to see him, sooner or later. I can't imagine how she will take it. Nobody ever knows how Lavinia will act, and she has not been normal since your father left home."

"Maybe he will come back when he knows I am here," Roy said hopefully.

"And maybe he won't. Anyhow, I shouldn't count on that. I'll leave the door ajar, so you can hear when I call you. But, for heaven's sake, don't let that child start crying."

She shuffled, rheumatically, out of the room, while Roy listened, with suspended breath, for the sound of a ponderous tread on the stairs. "Oh, God," breathed the girl mutely, "please make them give Timothy a chance."

# IV

**W**HEN she believed the past was over, Roy said to herself, it was merely hidden. What had happened here was still happening; the past was still going on, disjointed but alive, into the present, and from the present, on again, into the future. She remembered that evening, years before, when she seemed to feel the house breathe and stir in suspense, through its thin walls, while it waited with her for the coming of tragedy. Yet the pulse, then as now, was within herself; the vibrations flowed out from her own heart into the cast-off shapes of inanimate objects. Without me, she thought, there would be no suspense, no vibrations, and there would be, now, no tragic remembrance. I let life defeat me. I did what I chose to do. I must pay what I have to pay, without whimpering. But Timothy . . . Why should Timothy have to go on, all his life, paying for my love and my hate and for my revenge? Downstairs, in the room below this, Aunt Charlotte is telling Mother. At any minute, she may call to me, and then I must go down, and I must sit by Mother's bed, and she will ask me questions, and I shall have to answer them in lying words, or let my silence lie for me, until she has finished . . .

"Roy!" Charlotte's muffled voice was calling up the well of the staircase. "Roy, you may come down, and bring Timothy!"

"I can't go down, but I must," Roy told herself. "I must do what I cannot do."

Standing the drowsy child on his feet, she smoothed his rumpled curls and straightened the collar and shoulders of his jacket. Then, pushing away the moment, she hesitated, till Charlotte's imperative call floated up again from below.

"Come with me, darling. They are waiting for us." She had always talked to Timothy as if he were old enough to understand everything that she said. This was the reason, she felt, that sometimes he appeared to be more a small man than a little child. But the stairs to the third story were straight and steep, and while she helped him to descend, showing him where he must place his uncertain feet in blue shoes, she thought, with a clutch at her heart, after all he is only a baby.

An instant later, as she opened her mother's door, Roy was aware that she passed from the shelter of self-deception to an inescapable certainty. Though Lavinia was still wrapped in her silky cocoon of hypochondria, the pathetic illusion did not extend beyond the boundaries of her own personality. The years had washed over her and receded. Her puffed and livid skin was unlined; her pale bulging eyes, in hollowed sockets, were still the colour of over-ripe Malaga grapes. Even her old fashioned wrapper of purple challis might have been, and probably was, the same garment she had worn on that stormy August evening more than three years ago. In the first moment, Roy did not notice the softer day-bed, and the covers of bright chintz, which appeared oddly conspicuous in the shabby room. What was it Aunt Charlotte had said? Having money to spend had made Lavinia as close as the bark on a tree.

"So you've come back, my poor child." Holding out her arms, she raised her stayless figure on her pillows.

"Yes, Mother. Yes, I've come back."

"You look terribly ill. I should scarcely have known you." After they had kissed, Lavinia sank down and put her handkerchief to her eyes. "Is that why you came?"

"Yes. Yes, I suppose so. I had to go somewhere."

"I can't bear to see you so thin."

"As soon as she has enough to eat, she will pick up," Charlotte said, with sanguine hypocrisy.

"I've had pneumonia twice, but the doctor says I shall get well if I go away to be cured."

"Oh, my poor daughter! No wonder you are a wreck of yourself."

"I know I shall get well, Mother. If only you will take care of Timothy, I know I can get well."

"Timothy?" Lavinia, who had ignored the child as utterly as if he were a piece of luggage Roy had brought in and dropped, now turned a reluctant gaze in his direction. "Aunt Charlotte has told me," she murmured, in a hoarse whisper, "but I couldn't believe it. Not of a child of mine! I couldn't bring myself to believe it."

"It is true." Roy's lips stiffened. "Anything can be true of anybody. I am sorry I had to come home . . . I know just how you feel . . . Oh, but there was nothing else I could do! I had nowhere to go . . ."

"Of course, my child. Of course, you must have all the help we can give you. Isn't your mother the only person you could come to in trouble? There hasn't been a single hour in the last three years when I have not prayed for you in my heart."

"Then you will help me Mother?"

"Weren't you sure I would, Roy? Didn't you come straight to me?"

"Yes, I came. I came home."

"You knew you could depend on your family. We will think it all over, Aunt Charlotte and I, and decide what is best to be done. There are right and wrong ways of mending mistakes. No one need ever suspect what you've been through . . . or your . . . your trouble . . ." Her glance turned to Timothy, and then flinched sharply away. "We must find the poor child a good home. Louisa Littlepage is interested in placing orphans in good Christian homes. No one else need know. I can tell her that he is the child of a . . . a . . . of a refined refugee . . .

or, perhaps, of a relative who was killed in the war . . ."

Roy flung out her hand with a resentful gesture. "No. Oh, no . . ." she began, stormily, when the door opened without a warning sound, and a young and pretty undergraduate nurse appeared, bearing Lavinia's ample lunch on a tray.

"Miss Smithson is taking care of me, Roy," Lavinia explained, by way of introduction.

"Lunch will be ready in a few minutes," the nurse began. "Oh, what a darling child!"

"He is our little refugee," Lavinia said hurriedly. "His father was killed, and his mother is in a hospital. Roy has adopted him for the duration. Did you say his father was killed or missing, Roy?"

Roy nodded, in frozen surprise. "Missing," she replied stiffly. "Yes, he is missing."

Though Lavinia instinctively practised deceit, she wore a slightly mulish expression, as if the falsehood she uttered had done violence to her better nature.

Now she will have to keep him, Roy told herself, and the next instant: Oh, but she won't! She will find some excuse to pretend him away.

Having delicately arranged Lavinia's lunch on the table, the nurse bent over Timothy, who stood, shyly and awkwardly, gazing up at his grandmother. "You have the bluest eyes I ever saw. What is your name, little boy?"

The child's fascinated gaze dropped slowly from Lavinia's face to the lunch on the table.

"He knows his name perfectly," Roy broke in hastily. "You wouldn't believe that he can be a real chatterbox when he isn't with strangers . . . Tell the lady your name, Timmy," she added entreatingly.

Without looking at her, the child frowned and shook his head.

"I expect the cat has got his tongue," the nurse remarked, with her bright professional air. "Hasn't the cat got your tongue, little boy?"

"Kitty . . ." The name burst from Timothy's lips. "Timmy . . . Roy'l."

"He means 'Royal'," Roy explained. "Sometimes he stammers over his letters." At the crucial instant, the baby's faltering syllables had provided both an established family and a name.

"He looks bright. Of course, he is feeling shy in a new place."

"He is bright," Roy said proudly. "I could tell when he first began to think and to make up things in his mind."

"Well, he is a fine little man." The nurse smiled rapturously at Timothy, whose large, intensely blue eyes were fastened on his grandmother's tray. "I don't see how his mother could bear to part with him. But I expect you're both hungry. Come right downstairs. I'll have the chops broiled in a few minutes."

"B'ead." The child pointed solemnly to the roll Lavinia was breaking. "Budder. Mi'k. Meat." He held out his hand, and Lavinia, gravely reluctant, put a bit of crust into his pink curved palm, which tightened over it into a small, hard fist.

"He must be starved!" the nurse exclaimed, with ready sympathy. "How old did you say he is?"

"Two years and five months. He will soon be two and a half."

"Well, I think he's wonderful for his age. Boys are usually more backward than girls. You can give him his chicken gumbo, and I'll have the rest ready before you've finished."

"I'm going home now," Charlotte said, from the door, where she had lingered, "but I'll be straight back as soon as I've had a bite to eat. Is there anything I can do for you, Lavinia?"

"Nothing." Lavinia's tone was lugubrious, but she continued, with relish, to eat her chicken gumbo, and to spread butter plentifully on bits of roll. "Nothing, except call up Louisa

Littlepage and ask why she neglected to drop by this morning."

"So she hasn't come yet? Well, you must remember that she is hard-pressed for time. I don't see how she can keep up so many different activities. Now, that she's taken on the Red Cross, without giving up her social reforms, I suppose she will find her days too crowded for visiting."

"You may tell her I wish to see her about her orphanage."

"That will bring her, I know. Maybe you'll think of something else later. The child is famished, Roy. You'd better give him his lunch."

"I'll come back, Mother." Grasping Timothy's hand, as if she expected him to be seized and taken from her, Roy hurried out of the room, and followed Charlotte's sweeping gait down the stairs.

When the older woman had reached the hall below, she stopped, with her hand on the front door, and spoke in a cautious whisper: "You found your mother sadly under the weather? This has been a great shock to her."

"Isn't she always like this?"

"No. Oh, no. She has been happier this last year than I've ever seen her. So many people come to sit with her in the afternoon, and you know how she loves to talk about her complaints. There has been a great deal of sympathy for her, though, since the war started, she has not had so many visitors, and I think that has depressed her. But she takes everyone into her confidence, and you can't imagine the comfort she finds in Louisa Littlepage. Louisa was always an ardent feminist, and this seems to have grown upon her since her marriage so late in life. She has made quite a cause of your mother's side of the . . . well, of the separation."

"How is she . . . I mean, Mother . . . really taking it? I couldn't tell. Not in those few minutes."

"You wouldn't believe it," Charlotte's voice dropped still

lower, and she glanced apprehensively up the staircase, "but it has really made a new woman of her. It isn't William's legacy, and not having to worry about how much she spends, because she grows more saving every day. What has helped her is having a just grievance. It wasn't enough for her to feel ill-used. She wanted something solid to complain of, and now she has her real wrongs, and, what is more consoling, everybody knows she has them."

"Poor Father," Roy's lips formed the words silently, as Charlotte opened the door and went out.

In the dining-room light wavered and changed until it was like a room seen in memory. Thinking of her father, Roy felt the muscles of her throat tighten with pain. It was I who deserted him, she told herself, while she placed Timothy in a chair, on top of a dictionary and two cushions which the nurse had arranged for him. "That's right, Timmy, darling," she laughed at him through a mist. "Now, you're as high as the table."

But the child could not be diverted. "Hung'y," he insisted, thrumming gravely on the crocheted mat, which was frayed at the edges. Mother is better off, Roy thought, but nothing is different downstairs, except that everything is more dilapidated. She held a spoonful of jellied soup to Timothy's lips, and he swallowed it eagerly, and then held up his open rosy mouth, exactly, she said to herself, like a hungry robin. "But you must feed yourself, baby," she said presently, closing his fingers over the spoon. "You must learn to do things for yourself." Her eyes filled and then shone with her sudden smile. "You must learn not to expect help."

The young nurse tripped in breezily, with a flutter of animation. "The little man likes his milk, doesn't he? And he is eating nicely all by himself."

Roy had poured out the milk, and she pressed his hands

firmly round the stem of the cup, while he drank slowly, careful not to spill a drop, and holding tight with his greedy fingers. "He is learning to do everything for himself," she said, "even to put on his clothes. I am teaching him not to depend on other people."

"You're teaching him young." The white skirt rustled through the swinging door into the pantry. There was the sound of clinking dishes, and a little later an appetizing smell floated through the crack of the door, while Roy felt that the pit of her stomach expanded with emptiness. "Oh, how good you are!" she exclaimed. "It has been years since I smelt anything so delicious." Taking the glass from Timothy's careful hands, she began patiently showing him how to butter his bread with the small blunt knife.

"Good! Good!" Timothy cried, when the door swung back again, and the nurse flitted in with a dish of broiled chops. "I've cooked a little ground-up steak for the child. It is ground so fine, we shan't have to shred it for him . . . Make a good lunch, Mrs. Kingsmill. You both look as if you could do with a hearty meal."

At the sound of that unfamiliar name, twice repeated, Roy started and looked at her anxiously. So Mother gave me away to her, she thought. Then, collecting herself, she said aloud, "Yes, we both need something to eat. The eggnog Aunt Charlotte gave me was the first thing I had had since a sandwich for lunch yesterday."

The nurse was all bubbling sympathy. "I'm glad I fried some potatoes. Mrs. Timberlake likes them that way . . . Here's your good meat-ball, Timmy. But you must be careful not to drop anything on your nice knitted suit. You'd better let me fasten this napkin round your neck. That will make you feel easier." She broke into a twittering giggle. "I declare, I'm talking to him just as if he could take in every word . . . And there's a whole lovely cup of baked custard, with nutmeg all over the top. We saved that from Mrs. Timberlake's dinner last night . . ."

At last, the voice sank into a murmur, stopped for a restful instant, and then ran on again, as the nurse brought her own plate to the table, and sat down to her belated lunch.

"Mrs. Timberlake wants me to do an errand while you sit with her," she said. "Then I'll wash the dishes and tidy up before the new cook comes in . . . At least, I hope one will come in," she added doubtfully.

"Let me do the dishes," Roy begged. "I am used to that."

"Not on your life!" The nurse laughed the offer aside. "Why, you look as if you could be knocked flat by a feather." Her strong, brisk, tones rang out. How sanguine, how eager! Roy thought. How impervious to tragedy! The mad world might be devouring its children, but this one hard-working girl was avid for life.

Roy shrank slightly away. "I know I look wretchedly."

"Well, I've seen worse sights." The nurse was cheerful but candid. "Not that it would hurt you to put on a bit. Your face has gone a little too peaked. Don't you think you could manage another chop?"

"No, I'm stuffed." Roy's eyes filled with tears. "Why are you so good to me?"

"I'm not good, but you look down on your luck. I've been there myself. I think you were a brick, too, to take on that child. I suppose he was sent over."

"Yes, he was sent over. He was so young he does not remember it." That was the fault with a single lie, Roy told herself, whether it was your own or another's. One lie could not stand alone; it must be securely woven into an intricate system.

"Is his mother in England?"

"Yes, she is in England."

"It must be terrible for her, with his father missing. Has he ever seen his little boy?"

Roy glanced down at Timothy, who was scraping the nutmeg from the top of his custard. Even as a baby, he was unpredictable, and she could never tell how much he understood of what they were saying. "No," she answered, after a hesitation. "No, the child was born after he went away."

"Has he been long missing?"

"For nearly two years and a half. We think . . ." she bit off her words sharply, and went on in an expressionless voice. "We think he was killed or . . . or died in prison."

"How terrible! And she couldn't keep the child with her?"

"No. Oh, no, she couldn't keep him."

"Well, it's wonderful of you to take him. I'd like to do something as fine as that. If it wasn't for my mother, I'd go over with the Red Cross. But after my father died, I had to look after her. She has diabetes, and she has to take insulin."

"You are doing your job. I don't see why you should envy anyone else."

"That's what Mother tells me, but I can't help wanting a part in this war. Now, there's Mrs. Timberlake's bell. I'll go after her tray, and then I'll hurry up with the dishes before I start out on my errand. No, I don't need the least bit of help. Your mother wants you to sit with her. It was something terrible the way she missed you."

"But I was never her favourite." There was a flicker of surprise in Roy's glance from Timothy to the nurse. Had her mother really missed her? Or was the pretence merely a lesser symptom of hypochondria?

"You wouldn't think so if you'd heard her talk. There, she's ringing again! I guess I'd better be quick about answering it."

"Full!" Timothy exclaimed, clapping his hand on the spot where he felt the baked custard to be.

"Isn't it nice, Timmy, to be full once more?"

"Nice!" the child stretched himself, with a yawn. "Nice. Full. S'eepy."

"You may go fast asleep as soon as you've spoken to the lady upstairs. Don't you want to see the nice lady?"

"No . . . no . . . no . . ." At first, he resisted, pulling away from her with all his strength, but when she grasped him more firmly by the shoulders, he went with her obediently, though he clutched at the nurse's starched skirt, when she passed him on the stairs.

"Your mother is waiting for you, Mrs. Kingsmill. Timmy can have a good nap on the little couch." While the nurse sped cheerfully on her way, Roy dragged the unwilling child up the few steps and into Lavinia's room.

"What are you going to do with that child, Roy? I mean, now." Lavinia's voice was sharpened by exasperation. "How much does he understand?"

"Of course, he wouldn't have any idea of what we are talking about . . . But I think, he would be better upstairs. He is on edge from the trip."

"Then take him up to your room. I must have a talk with you before Charlotte comes back."

The child was already at the closed door, beating angrily against it with his tiny fists. "Go, Mama! Go! Ugly!" he cried furiously. In the very beginning, Roy said to herself unhappily, he had, through some babyish instinct of repugnance, estranged the only living person who was able to help him.

"You must be good, Timmy," she whispered urgently, as they climbed, step by step, to the third floor. By the time she had lifted him to the bed, his rage had died down, and he was again nodding. "Be good," she repeated, almost fiercely. How could the mind of so young a child become the battleground of inherited antipathies? "Will you be good, Timmy?" she asked.

"G-o-o-d!" Timothy echoed the word after her, before he thrust a defiant thumb into his mouth. Then, as he was about to drop off, he jerked the thumb from his lips, and piped in an urgent treble: "B-a-d!"

She looked down on him through eyes that were bright with anxiety. What perverse streak in his nature made him, in the same moment, so difficult and so gentle? Had his unknown father survived in his gentleness or in his perversity? How could she ever know what to expect of him? How could she be sure either of his likeness to herself or of his differences? All she could hope to do was to feel her way toward some unpredictable truth; and, even when she encountered truth, should she be able to recognize it by the touch alone?

When she covered him with the blue blanket, he was already asleep. Removing his thumb from his mouth, without waking him, she pressed it against his side . . . A minute later, as she leaned out to close the green shutters, a flight of pigeons scared off from the house-top, and circled, in a continuous curve, over the distant roofs. The air in the room stirred and softened, while a thin golden light filtered in through the drawn slats. I shall have to leave him, she thought. Mother must help us, and it will spoil everything if she takes a dislike to him.

After she has fastened the shutters, she lingered for a moment over his bright head and his hidden eyes. So his father had lain, she remembered, with the unshielded candour of sleep in his face and his attitude, when she had left him and gone out, alone, into the wan glimmer of daybreak.

# V

A S SHE entered the room, Lavinia received her with an air of doleful anticipation. "Now, tell me what this means, Roy. Tell me before Aunt Charlotte and the nurse come in."

Roy shook her head. "I can't tell you, Mother. I don't know what anything means."

"After all the trouble I've had . . ." Lavinia felt in her knitting-bag for a handkerchief and dabbed at her reddened eyelids.

"I'm sorry. I know I oughtn't to have come home."

"That is not an answer. Why did you do this, Roy?"

"It is the only answer I have, Mother. I don't know why I did it. I shall never know. But for Timothy, I could tell myself it never happened, and I could believe that."

"You couldn't possibly have cared for this man. You knew nothing about him."

Again Roy shook her head, in defiant perplexity. "Nothing. Oh, no, I did not care for him. If I had cared for him, it would not have happened . . ."

"You're talking pure nonsense. Charlotte says it was pity. She says pity went to your head . . . and . . . and . . ."

"That sounds silly, no matter who says it. Yet, perhaps . . . You could never understand, Mother. I can't understand myself, but it was mostly desperation, and a breaking away . . . Oh, but there's no use in talking about it, Mother, you must promise to keep Timothy till I am cured and come back for him."

Lavinia sighed. "Do you know, my dear, that I am an ill woman?"

"I am sorry, Mother. I haven't anybody else in the world to leave him with. Couldn't you engage somebody to look after him. Already, he is learning to do things for himself . . . And it will not be for long."

"I am obliged to keep two nurses," Lavinia continued, as if Roy had not spoken. "I am not able to leave my bed, except to move into this room in the morning, and to go back at night. I cannot cross the floor without help."

"He wouldn't bother you, Mother."

"You haven't any idea how the cost of living has increased. What with the war and these new taxes growing worse all the time, I can barely manage to make two ends meet." She dived into her knitting-bag and retrieved, from the jumble of odds and ends, a dingy stocking she had half finished. "You can't even get wool any longer. I had to ravel out an old slumber robe to find this yarn."

"But I must have help, Mother. I must have help."

Lavinia dropped her knitting, while she turned a bleak, compassionate gaze on her daughter. "Of course, you shall have all the help I can give you. There isn't any sacrifice I shouldn't make gladly for any one of my children. You know how I love you. Unless Doctor Buchanan can tell us of a better place, you must go straight up to the Adirondacks. And you must not worry about that child. The nurse will be sure to repeat what I said to her, and it doesn't sound nearly so incredible as it would have sounded before the war. So many people on James River have adopted refugees for the duration . . ."

"But, Mother . . . Oh, Mother, please listen . . ."

"No, Roy, you will only excite yourself. It is very bad for your complaint. You might even bring on a hemorrhage."

"If you would only let me tell you!"

"No, you must not tell me. Can't you think of my heart? Haven't I enough to bear without this?"

"I know, Mother, I know." Roy turned her face away, while broken coughs shuddered through her. "If only I could think of some other way!" She flung out her thin arm in a helpless gesture.

"I am thinking more of you than of myself, Roy. Who can feel for a child as a mother does? The little boy will have the very best care. Louisa Littlepage has a conscience too big for her body. She would place him in a fine Christian home; and it isn't necessary for her to know any more than we have already told the nurse. Timothy Royal . . . That is his name."

"No, no, Mother. That's just his baby way of speaking. I am trying to teach him to say his name properly, but strangers confuse him, and he forgets all but Timmy."

"Well, it sounded like Royal. That's a good old Virginian name."

"I cannot give him up, Mother. I will take him and go away before I'll let Mrs. Littlepage have him."

"Where would you go, dear?"

Roy started and looked round the room to the window, as if she were seeking an escape from the question. "I'll go . . . I'll go . . . anywhere."

Lavinia's face became livid, while her hand flew to her damaged heart. "This will yet be the death of me. You have lived so recklessly, my child, that you have lost sight of the way all conservative, I may say all decent families still look upon such scandals. Though standards have relaxed, even in Queenborough, we have not completely lost our moral sense. Certain sins are still frowned upon . . ."

"I won't give him up, Mother. I won't . . . I won't . . ."

"Wait till you are well, Roy, to decide that. Your first duty is to go away and get well."

"How can I get well when I am worrying about Timothy?"

Lavinia heaved a patient sigh as she picked up her knitting. "I hope the British Relief will be able to use these stockings," she said, with subdued palpitations and recovered breath, "but the yarn feels as if it would give way. When you are in the sanatorium, my dear, why don't you do some serious work for the Red Cross? You might promise to knit a number of stockings if the wool is supplied." When Roy did not answer, Lavinia began, slowly and carefully, to pick up some dropped stitches. "It isn't," she said, with unconscious malice, "as if the child really belonged in the family."

"But he does, Mother. He is my child. He is your grandson just as much as if . . . as if . . ."

"I cannot feel that way, my daughter. Aunt Charlotte, though she holds some unconventional opinions, must share my belief. I hate to use harsh words, when you have been through so much, but we could never feel that a child born out of marriage is a member of—of our connection. I do not wish to speak ill of the dead, but we cannot deny that Uncle William indulged in loose living. Nobody knows how many children he might have had, here and there. But his marriage with Aunt Charlotte was childless, and his family strain expired at his death."

"It is unfair!" Roy cried, and the choking violence in her tone brought a gasp of pain from her mother. "It is unjust to punish the innocent!"

"That is true, but you should have remembered it sooner."

"Oh, I know. I know it is my fault. But I want Timothy. I can't simply not want him."

"If there were any possible way, Roy, I'd try to take him . . . at least till you are well . . . or the war is over. But my life hangs by a thread. What can you expect of an ill woman?"

"I know, Mother. I am sorry I had to bring this on you. If I hadn't thought Father was here . . . "

Lavinia flinched, while her natural expression was blotted out by a spasm of pain. "Hasn't Aunt Charlotte told you?"

"Yes. Yes, she had to tell me. I made her. It was the last thing I expected."

"Everybody says that." Lavinia bit her lower lip as if she were trying to keep back a moan.

"Of course, he had a mean life," Roy answered, defensively, "but I thought he would stick to it. I never dreamed he would do this."

"It wasn't as if I had not been a good wife." In spite of her bitten lip, a sob burst from Lavinia, while she fumbled for the handkerchief she had again lost in her knitting bag. "I have searched my conscience, but I cannot honestly blame myself."

"I suppose he couldn't bear being idle, especially in wartime . . . but, even then . . ."

"But we had more to live on than he had ever earned. Why wasn't he content to spend his declining years quietly with me? As it is, I've had to have in an extra nurse at night, and that puts a strain on my income."

"It was being dependent. Father could never stand being dependent. You remember how he was about Uncle William."

"But Uncle William is dead. No, it was more than that. I never trusted Kate Oliver."

"Oh, but you can't mean! Nobody could think . . ."

Lavinia had found her handkerchief and was patting her moist face. Was she actually enjoying the situation? Roy wondered. Was Aunt Charlotte right, after all, and could a solid grievance fill the hollow vacancy of frustration? "You don't know what people are saying," Lavinia replied, at the end of a depressed silence.

"Aren't they both too old to start gossip? I mean, of course, to make a scandal. Father is over sixty-three, and Mrs. Oliver must be nearly fifty-five. It sounds ridiculous to imagine . . ."

Lavinia raised her eyes with the look of an unwilling martyr. "You are young, Roy. It is like Louisa Littlepage, who is as thin as a wafer, insisting that Kate Oliver is too fat for a love affair. When you are older, you will learn that people are never too old or too fat to cause a scandal."

"I don't care," Roy rejoined defiantly. "I do not believe it. Mrs. Oliver must have needed an overseer."

Lavinia frowned. "She could have found someone else. There are other elderly men out of work. But you don't know Kate Oliver as I do. She has had her eye on Asa since her husband died more than ten years ago."

Roy laughed, with a hint of scorn in her tone. "Well, I shan't believe that Father ever had his eye on her . . . not in that way." Meeting her mother's protruding gaze, she thought: But I don't understand. I know Mother is good, after her fashion, and I know Father is good too. Yet she does not like people to think him good. She wishes them to think he is bad.

"No, I never trusted Kate Oliver," Lavinia repeated. "Some people says she spends her time doing good, but what does she make out of it? She keeps a lot of lame ducks down on her farm, and you can't make me believe she doesn't get a day's work out of every one of them. She isn't running that farm for charity, any more than she's taken on your father because they both wanted a part in this war."

"It was my fault. Father wouldn't have gone if he had known I was coming back."

"You were always his favourite." The words were strangled in Lavinia's throat, and she went on with a catch in her voice: "He would have done anything in the world for you. But you never let us know even that you were alive."

"It sounds cruel, but I did not mean to be cruel . . . The

truth was I didn't think . . . not for a moment." No, she had not thought, Roy told herself reproachfully. Or she had thought only of her own life and of Timothy's. Had she been more ungrateful than other children? Or was youth always like that, self-seeking, over-confident, heedless of any pain that it caused? "Father would do anything in the world for me," she said desperately. "He couldn't stay away if he knew I was in trouble."

"If I could really feel that way, Roy."

"Oh, but he couldn't, Mother. Hasn't he always done what I wanted? Do you remember when I was little, and had diphtheria? He stayed away from work, and shut himself up with me on the third floor. I wouldn't let anybody else touch me. I've forgotten all about that time, except that I was dying of terror till Father held me."

Lavinia's eyes were humid with recollection. "That was when Stanley was born. You can't possibly remember it."

"But I do. Just that. My terror, and Father holding me." Roy shut her eyes tight, while she tried in vain to release the closed vision. Did she really remember it? Or was her memory still too faint to retain an indelible picture? Anyhow, she thought, I cannot go back beyond Father. Father is always there from the beginning.

When she opened her eyes, it seemed to her that the light in the room was moving in circles. In a slowly revolving centre, her mother's look was suspended, alone, unsupported, but filled with a heart-broken loneliness. Some message outside herself, Roy felt, was struggling to reach her, to break through the hardened shell of identity, or of repugnance. Poor Mother, she has suffered . . . but the words were as hollow as blown bubbles. Poor Mother, she has never known love, and love was perhaps, the one thing she wanted from life. While Roy gazed at Lavinia's mauve-tinted features, she reminded herself, with detached pity, of her mother's frustrated girlhood. To desire, and not ever to be desired, that, Roy suspected, without knowing, was the hidden core of the tragedy. To be without charm in a place and a period when charm alone was important in women. Perhaps, in the beginning, she had tried sweetness, and when sweetness failed her, she had transferred her hunger for love into a craving for power. For it was power, not love, not loneliness, not even vain longing, that had fed and thrived upon distrust and jealousy, and upon real or fancied affronts.

But what of me? asked Lavinia's look. Haven't I felt unhappiness? Haven't I been deserted?

"Father will come back if I ask him," Roy said, with confidence. "I know he will come back for me."

A gleam shone in Lavinia's eyes. "If he would come to take care of the child . . . Then people might never know." The gleam was drowned in a surge of resentment. "Charlotte said he looked happy." Her tone was edged with suspicion. "She said she had never seen him so happy."

"But his life is over. How could anyone begin life at sixty-three . . . Or is he nearly sixty-five?"

"He was sixty-three his last birthday. Charlotte said he appeared satisfied, as if he had what he wanted." It seemed to Roy that her mother's expression curdled with bitterness. "I suppose she meant he wanted Kate Oliver."

"But she couldn't have said that to you. Not Aunt Charlotte."

Lavinia shook her head. "I have always known Aunt Charlotte did not like me. She tried to turn Uncle William against me."

"That isn't a bit like her. But I don't care what anybody says . . . Father would come home if he knew how I needed him."

"If you feel that way," Lavinia was hesitating over her idea, "why don't you ask him?"

"You mean he may come here? I may ask him to come here?"

"Not while he is with Kate Oliver. Not until he has left her."

Roy sprang to her feet, trembling with eagerness. "Oh, but I'll go down to the farm! It is still early. I can go and get back before dark."

Lavinia's anger had softened, and the look of reluctant martyrdom closed down over her features. "I am not sure, Roy, that it is right for you to go. I have told you as much as I thought wise . . . but, even then, there are things I felt it was better to leave unsaid."

What was her mother trying to tell her? Something or nothing? Had they ever understood each other? Did human beings ever know the truth about one another? Perhaps she has suffered more than I suspected, Roy told herself. When we imagined ourselves superior, were we merely ignorant and undiscerning? When we behaved as secret enemies, were we simply strangers who might have become friends?

"Don't go, Roy. Not yet," Lavinia was pleading.

"I must, Mother. I must see for myself. There is no other way."

"But you will remember what I told the nurse? You will not let anyone know?"

"About Timothy? Oh, I shall have to tell Father. I must tell Father the truth."

"It is too far for you to go." Lavinia was sobbing under her breath. "And, after all, what is the use? Your father has left me."

"He will come back. I know he will come back with me."

"How will you go down? There are so few cars left. Even Aunt Charlotte cannot get tires for her car."

"There is still a bus, isn't there? I'll go on the bus, and I'll take Timothy. He will enjoy it."

"Roy, promise me you will be careful. I should die if you let people know." The printed frill was fluttering over Lavinia's heart. "This will yet be the end of me."

While she watched her, Roy's sympathy hardened. "I wish I'd stayed away, Mother."

"But you are here now."

"I can go away."

"Oh, I don't mean that. I want to help you, only you must try to understand what it means to me."

"I do know," Roy answered impatiently. "How could I help knowing?"

"I am trying to protect you, my poor child."

"To protect me!" Roy laughed. "Who can ever protect anyone else?" She turned at the door and looked back. "I am going now, Mother."

Lavinia's anxious gaze strained after her. "If only you will be careful, Roy. Try to be very careful if you see Craig."

"Craig!" Roy's figure drooped with a sudden shiver. "Why should I see Craig?"

"Are you cold, daughter?"

"No. No, I'm not cold . . . But why should you begin talking about Craig? Craig has gone out of my life. Craig isn't anything to me," she added fiercely. "Not anything in the world."

"There's no need to be violent. All I mean is . . . do not tell him about Timothy."

"I shan't see him. I can always avoid him."

"Well, you may run across him. Queenborough is a small place. But, if you do see him, take my advice. Do not tell him."

"About Timothy?"

"Yes, of course, I mean, don't let anyone tell him about the child."

"Why shouldn't I tell him?" Roy tossed her head with a challenging gesture.

"No matter how radical a man is," Lavinia said stiffly, "he cannot take a thing like that from a woman. Not if he ever cared for her."

"He never loved me. I wasn't a woman to him. I was a lost cause."

"Well, you cared for him. You were going to marry him."

"He meant safety. After Peter, I wanted security . . . Yes, I cared for him, because he made me feel safe. I mean, safe from life. I had been torn in pieces . . . Oh, but there isn't any safety in love!" And she thought: If I loved Craig because he promised security, I loved Peter because he meant uncertainty and wildness and danger, and not ever seeing round the next corner. Was love or life always like that? Did first love seek wildness in adventure? Was it only last love that sought security in contentment? But, beyond the seeking, when one had lost both adventure and contentment, what was left to fall back upon, to stand guard before? "When did you see Craig?" she asked abruptly, with her hand on the door-knob.

Lavinia hesitated. "It must have been a year ago. Perhaps longer than that. He dropped by to ask if I'd heard from you. He seemed to feel we should go into the war, sooner or later, and he was depressed because he could not get into the Navy. You remember how he always dragged one foot a little."

"Yes, I know. He limped so slightly, I thought it rather appealing."

"There was a nervous condition too. This affected his eyes. He told me he was ordered to stop drinking and to build up his health. I haven't seen him since then, but Louisa Littlepage met him at a Red Cross meeting, and he told her his eyes were all right again."

"Well, I'm glad," Roy replied coldly. "Then there's less danger of my running across him."

"No, I don't suppose you will see him, though he used to be one of Kate Oliver's lame ducks. But if you should see him . . ."

"Oh, I shan't tell him! Why should I tell him? He is nothing to me."

"Then he isn't likely to hear it . . . not if he is well again, and is in the Navy. After all, nobody knows what may happen before this war ends and he comes home."

"Anyhow, I shan't be here." There was a quiver of anger in Roy's tone. "Now, I've really gone, Mother. I know Father will come back with me."

Her martyred smile, stricken before it was born, flattened Lavinia's mouth. "Not unless he has left Kate Oliver . . ."

Running up the stairs, Roy thought, in perplexity: She does not want to give up her grievance. Oh, but poor Mother, her grievance is the only living thing she has left.

# VI

A T THE top of the stairs Roy stopped, while fear clutched at her nerves. If I were to die, who would take Timothy? What would happen to Timothy if I were to die? She could feel the dark terror hammering in her mind, and drumming on into the hidden places of consciousness. Her whole life was now centered in one small helpless figure. Traditions might topple over, the world might crash in ruins about her; but Timothy must be saved . . .

She opened the door softly, and found the child sitting up in bed, with his wide fixed gaze on the screen of leaves at the window. "Birdie, Mama. Mine." Only within the last few months, after his second birthday, had he discovered the dawning sense of possession. He had learned to say "mine" and "yours"; and she had wondered whether all children began, at this early age, to distinguish between themselves and the objects around them. Or was this trait merely an infant manifestation of Fitzroy acquisitiveness?

Standing here beside the bed, following the child's rapt gaze after the pigeons, she asked herself, yet once again, why this should have happened to her, and why, having happened, it had changed nothing? Timothy was the last thing she had wanted, while she was running away from her life; and now that Timothy had come, he was the last thing she would ever consent to let go. In seeking a way out of the past, she had plunged deeper into the wilderness that was, and was not, herself . . . "Still, the worst has not happened," she said, speaking aloud: "The worst thing would be to lose courage. As long as I am not afraid, I can face anything."

At her voice, which sounded as far away as bells chiming, Timothy turned and looked up into her face. "Go, Mama," he begged, while he crawled to the edge of the bed and tried to climb over. "Mama, go." His pleasure in the pigeons was over, and he was knitting his small blank forehead into an angry frown. "Go . . . go . . . ," he urged impatiently, as she lifted him to the floor.

"Yes, darling, we're going. We're going to see Grandfather." Slipping his arms into the sleeves of his jacket, and smoothing back his bright, tumbled hair, she added, with firmness: "But you must be good, Timmy, you must be good."

He waited, obediently, while she carefully pulled on his cap and straightened the tassel over his left ear. Then, seizing a fold of her short skirt, he tried to drag her away from the mirror, before she had settled her hat at the right angle. "Go, go, go—o . . ."

"Be quiet, Timmy, or the lady downstairs will hear you." She turned to pick up her coat and her purse, which she had tossed down on the bed that used to be Peter's. But I haven't enough money, she reminded herself, in dismay. I shall have to ask Mother for money. Downstairs, a bell rang, and she thought, while a wave of relief rushed over her, that must be Aunt Charlotte. It will be easier asking Aunt Charlotte.

"Go, go, go-o-o." Timothy chanted under his breath, as he ran ahead of her to the landing.

"Wait, Timothy, you must let Mother help you." Reaching after him as he started down, she hurried, step by step, to the second floor, and then down again to the front hall, where Mrs. Fitzroy was assembling her efforts before she mounted the flight of stairs.

"Oh, Aunt Charlotte, you've come just when I need you!"

The old woman eased herself in her stays. "Why, what's the matter, my dear? Has anything worse happened?"

"No. Yes . . . I haven't any money." Roy glanced at Timothy's feet, which were gingerly feeling their way down the two lowest steps. "I am going to see Father, and I haven't enough money for my way on the bus."

"You mean you're going to Hunter's Fare? But your mother . . ."

"She doesn't mind. She wants me to bring Father back with me."

"Then she has had a change of heart. Well, I've plenty of money for you. I just stopped by the bank." Mrs. Fitzroy groped about in her vast bag and brought out an oblong brown envelope. "Here, take it all, Roy. I cashed a cheque for fifty dollars, and I haven't had time to spend it." A beam of satisfaction shone over her features. After all, for a widow of ample income, munificence was, no doubt, the simplest and the least exacting solution of any problem. As long as she was not required to give up her new freedom or to change her manner of living, she was ready, Roy felt, to deal bountifully with a situation she had not made, and for which no one, not even Uncle William, could have held her responsible.

Roy's lip quivered. "You're good to me. Does the bus still run by the corner?"

"Yes, I saw it as I turned in. That baby isn't big enough to do much walking. Be sure to ask the conductor to change you at the right James River stop. Somebody—it may have been Craig—told me they had put on a new bus that goes near Hunter's Fare."

"Craig?" Roy repeated in a smothered voice. She felt that the muscles of her face ached from smiling.

"I hadn't meant to tell you. Not that it matters now . . . But I ran across Craig one day in the bank. He told me he was all right again, and he is going into the Navy. I thought he looked very well."

"Mother told me. I hope he has gone."

"He may have." Charlotte looked at her searchingly. "But if you should see him . . . oh, Roy, please be careful."

"That's what Mother said. She is afraid I may tell him about Timothy."

"Well, she is right, for once . . . But the most important thing, now, is to cure that cough. I will help as much as I can." Her face appeared to flatten out and to dissolve in an oleaginous flood of pity. "I will do anything in the world for you, except take care of a child. At my age," she repeated emphatically, "that is expecting too much of me."

"Mother feels the same way. And Timothy wouldn't be happy here. He hates it already. I couldn't leave him unless . . . unless Father comes back."

Charlotte sighed. "Well, I have warned you against counting on that. He is like a man released from prison . . . or he was when I saw him."

"We were all selfish, I know. But Timothy is different. He is only a baby." Her voice hardened, as if she were steeling her mind against tenderness. "I will call you when I come in, Aunt Charlotte. Either Father or I will call you."

As the door shut behind her, sunshine blazed in her eyes. Holding fast to Timothy's hand, she helped him down the front steps to the street, which was littered with fallen red and yellow leaves from the maples. Impatience jerked at her muscles, and she sighed helplessly, when, after faltering on for a few steps, the child stopped, whimpered once, and sat down in the middle of the pavement. "Timmy's ti'ed."

"Oh, darling, it is such a little way. Can't you walk it to help Mama? Then we'll get into the bus, and we'll go away to pick flowers and to see birds, and . . . and . . ." She broke off with a choking sound, and sobered by her tone, the child struggled to his feet and trotted on at her side. While he trudged bravely over the uneven bricks, she thought, almost in tears: He is worn out, and he is only a baby . . . How could she possibly find a way to carry him from the road gate to the house at Hunter's Fare? How could he walk that far on his small tired feet? But she would not think of that till she was facing the road and the danger. Perhaps someone would be passing. Perhaps a farmer would stop and pick them up on his way from the station. So many times, when she was caught in a desperate plight, some fortunate accident intervened . . .

Of a sudden, without evident cause, fear, dark, nameless, undefined, rushed into her thoughts. Stooping, she caught the startled child to her bosom. Then, meeting the terror-stricken look in his face, she forced a playful smile to her lips. "Who is the beautiful baby?" she asked gaily, as she used to ask so often when he was learning his first words.

For a moment, after she released him, he drew back and stood watching her, in solemn-eyed wonder. Slowly as her smile grew more natural, the wonder faded into a glimmer of recognition. "I is," he said shyly.

Those were his earliest syllables. They were the first words, linked together, that divided his identity from the animate and inanimate objects around him. She had feared he was backward —the memory tore at her heart—when he had surprised her, one morning, by lisping softly, in answer to her question, "I is."

"Oh, Timmy, I cannot let you go . . . I cannot . . . I cannot . . ."

A man hurrying by, stopped and turned back. "Are you in trouble, lady? Can I help you?"

He looks kind, she told herself. Oh, but it is extraordinary the way strangers so often come, at the right moment, to help you, when your friends, and even your family, let you down. Aloud, she said: "He is too tired to walk. We must catch the bus at the corner."

"Then we'd better run for it. It's wartime, and there's a long wait between buses."

He snatched up the child, and together they raced down the block to the corner. An omnibus had stopped at the curb, and he pushed her up the step, before he lifted in Timothy. "Oh, thank you!" she cried, but the man had already disappeared under the trees.

"Yes, strangers are kind," she said in a whisper, while she settled Timothy in her lap and pressed his sleepy head down on her arm.

# PART TWO
## Afternoon: The Substance

# I

THE great oak at the cross-roads was beginning to turn. Half-green, half-russet, the higher sunlit branches were veined with bright wine-colour, while the lower boughs were still darkened by bluish shadows. That tree is like Father, Roy thought. Everything is against it, but some inner strength holds it together.

Since the change at the omnibus station, the child had slept quietly in her arms, and awaking now with a start, he asked, in surprise, "Home!"

"No, darling. Not home, but a nicer place. We've come to see your . . ." She bit off her words, remembering Lavinia. "We've come to the pretty country."

His forehead puckered under his ruffled hair, and she wondered what her reply had meant to him, and how much or how little he had understood. After twisting from side to side, he sat up, refreshed and interested, while she searched the small scattered crowd in front of the country store. There were a few dusty cars, with dried mud caking the wheels, and, beside one of these, she recognized the animated shapes of two brown and white pointers. They're Pat and Percy, she told herself, with a thrill of pleasure. Father must have come for me. But when she hastened, clasping Timothy's hand, across the sunny space, she saw that the man coming toward her was not her father, but Craig Fleming.

A chill dumbness flooded her thoughts. Once again, she breathed the sharp earthy smells of that August night. She felt the storm in her face; she heard the rush of wind, the pattering sound under the trees; and she saw the crooked boughs of the

63

sycamore tossing, thirstily, in the rain. But that was all over, and finished. That was only a storm, without and within, which had lived and died more than three years ago.

"Well, Roy!"

"Oh, Craig!"

That was all. There was nothing more to be said. Never would there be anything more for them to say to each other. Looking beyond him, she tried to fix her eyes and her mind upon the visible world. A single leaf dropped from the highest bough of the great oak, and was spinning slowly down through the sunlight. Farther on, a narrow white road ran between level fields of scrub pine, broomsedge, and life-ever-lasting . . .

"Your father would have come," Craig said, "but he was obliged to keep an eye on the farm. We've had a bad time this year sowing our winter wheat and oats. Only the lame, the halt, and the half-blind will work in the country."

So that, of course, was what really mattered! Winter wheat and oats came first, even with her father.

"Mrs. Fitzroy telephoned." Craig was tanned and slightly coarsened in feature, and he was wearing overalls of faded blue denim over a rumpled shirt. There was a change in him, Roy said to herself, though she could not define it. Only his light roving eyes in his dark face were startlingly alive and unaltered.

"Yes?"

"She told us you had brought home a refugee." His glance turned to the child. "Attractive little chap, isn't he?" A furrow deepened between his eyebrows, and she caught a sudden slant of anxiety—or was it of understanding. He is afraid, she thought. He is afraid I may become tragic. How men dread the revival of an old tragedy!

Looking away from him, she stooped to pat the two pointers. "Yes," she repeated, vaguely disturbed. "Do you see the nice doggies, Timothy?"

"Doggies!" Timothy exclaimed, rapturously, "Woof!

Woof!" before he trotted off between Pat and Percy toward the dusty Ford.

"You don't mind my overalls?" Craig asked, and his tone was so vacant that she knew he was trying to fill in the awkward pause. "I have been tinkering with a harrow."

"Are you living at Hunter's Fare?"

"I have been there all summer. Anybody who can wield a pitchfork is welcome on any farm. I make a poor substitute for a hired man, but it seems more useful than law. Next week," he added bluntly, "I go into the Navy."

"Oh, but your eyes?"

"They were turned down once, but that was before Pearl Harbor. I was ordered to work out-of-doors and to put on twenty pounds. Now, I'm fit again, if I'm ever likely to be."

Roy laughed, without merriment. Suddenly, the moment rang hollow, and she felt that she wanted to turn and run away, before time again came to life. "I wonder how Father looks in overalls," she said lightly. "Does he wear them?"

Craig's face cleared, and she told herself that flippancy was the right note. "Yes, we have gone native. War without a uniform releases the natural man." A faintly malicious smile flickered on his tight lips. "We have flung manners with the humanities overboard. We have abandoned the poor old classics because they do not make killers."

"It isn't easy to think of you and Father as killers."

"That's our trouble. We are both misfits in war. And we can't fool ourselves. We know killing is a dirty job, but in a dirty world somebody has to take on the dirty jobs."

"Is Father well? Is he happy?" She walked quickly to the car, where Timothy was climbing over the wheels.

"He is well. Who is happy?"

"Aunt Charlotte thinks he is happy . . . or has found something better than happiness."

"What," Craig retorted, "could be better than happiness?"

"I don't know. I haven't found it." Impatiently, she quickened her steps. Why did Craig have to come, when he only made everything harder?

With a wheezing snort, the decrepit car ploughed through the ragged weeds and lurched into the cross-road. "This bus," Craig said, proudly mocking, "has been known to burn up fifteen miles in an hour."

"It seems ridiculous, doesn't it?" How long, Roy wondered, could it go on, this tactful skating over the surface of life?

The autumn landscape broke apart and dissolved in a mist. Looking away from him, she gazed over the wide, flat fields, where the two pointers were leaping through the tall broom-sedge and life-ever-lasting. When the plumes of wheaten-red or silver-white stirred and divided, a few startled crows skimmed in flapping curves over their transparent shadows. In the windy brightness of October the movement of the distance was like the motion of ruffled water, of water rising and falling and breaking into waves of foam before it parted and scattered.

After a hot and humid summer, the season of 1942 was less brilliant than other autumns on James River. Through a haze of memory, she saw the pale, sad yellow, that tinge of disenchantment, which spread over the near meadows and the thinning border of woods. Then a finger of sunshine picked out the gold in hickories, beeches, and poplars, and the topmost boughs became a part of the changing light. Yes, the fall is sad here, she thought, but it is happy too. There was a wistful quality in the air, in the fall of the leaves, even in the slow, faint shadows of the crows drifting over an old cornfield.

In silence, except for the spasmodic efforts of the car, they wound between stretches of fallow land, cut sharply into a dark belt of pines, and bumped over a sunken road, through a field of fodder in shocks . . . Was Craig merely detached and indifferent? Or was there in his voice a note of direct hostility? Not that anything mattered. There were other things in life more important than loving. Not ever again, she clasped her child tighter, would she over-value the meaning of love . . . Lifting her eyes, she watched a flight of wild geese, travelling in a V-shaped wedge toward the South. "Oh, look, Timmy! Look up in the sky! Do you hear them, *honk, honk?*"

"Birdies!" Timothy cried, clapping his hands. "Up! Up! Up-pity!"

Craig followed her long upward gaze. "There aren't many geese going by this season. That is the largest flock I have seen. But others may be now on the way."

"Do they come down to rest?"

"Not yet. They must have flown inland for food. In the late afternoon they will fly back toward water."

"They look happy."

"Perhaps we look happy to them." He nodded toward a field of young green. "That's alfalfa putting up. We've had four cuttings this year. But we lost a part of it for lack of hands."

"There is so much yellow-green everywhere."

"Those are soy-beans. All the farmers are raising soy-beans and alfalfa. Both are easy and cheap. We had, too, a good pea-nut crop. The Government made us raise more peanuts than we could harvest." His tone was curiously impersonal, as if he were addressing an unseen audience. Without glancing at Roy, he nodded toward a field of harvested peanuts, each separate rick supported and held upright by a pole in the center, which gave it an odd resemblance to a human figure in a dark brown cloak. Huddled in groups of two or three, the peanut-ricks were like little hunchbacked men and women, all bowed and gossip-ing together . . . But we are wasting time, Roy told herself. If only we could go faster, and I could have the afternoon over and finished! What do I care about farming, when Timothy's whole future depends on the next hour or two?

But Craig, apparently, was indifferent to time. Already, the pointers were far ahead on their way home, now plunging up and down in the fields, now darting out into the road and casting back impatient glances at the slow-moving car. When, at last, Craig stopped before the red gate of Hunter's Fare, Roy saw, beyond the gate, a straggling and badly damaged procession of old cedars.

"How far is the house?" she asked.

"Half a mile. The approach used to be good."

"Shall I open the gate?"

For a long moment, while Roy waited in urgent silence, Craig did not reply. Around them, there was the low, perpetual humming of autumn, the vibration of innumerable small voices. The wind had turned, and they were sheltered by the huge overhanging boughs of the cedars. Through the sifting pollen of milkweed, Roy looked eagerly down the white road ahead, where Pat and Percy raced homeward. On the left, in an endless meadow, sheep were cropping lazily among uninterested cattle.

"Good God, Roy," Craig exclaimed, under his breath. "You look as if you had been on the rocks!"

"Oh, but it is over. Does anything that is over really matter?"

"Why did you come here? I mean, come to Hunter's Fare."

"Does that matter?"

"Well, doesn't it?"

"Not to you." The wild geese trailed, as faint as a pattern of blown smoke, over the marshes.

"Not much, perhaps . . ." Craig bent his scowling glance on the road. For an uncertain instant, he appeared to be starting the car; then his hand relaxed its grasp and slipped from the wheel.

"Shall I open the gate?" Roy asked again.

"Not yet. No, not yet." His gaze left the road, and he looked at her with hard and unyielding eyes. "You came home," he said, "because you had reached a dead end. There was nothing to do but turn back."

She drew sharply away. "We cannot ever turn back. Not to the past . . . We can only turn back on ourselves." An unnatural glow burned in her cheeks, and her hollowed eyes were suddenly dark with remembrance.

"So you came back," he said, "just as you went away, to escape. Weren't we always trying, you and I, to escape from personality? Weren't we forever running, round and round, in a blind circle? All of us. I do not mean you alone. I mean, every last one of us."

"Oh, but we always come back."

The furrows deepened between his eyebrows. "Like the tiger or the murderer, I suppose. We come back to the place where we have killed something."

"No, not that. We come back to our roots . . . Anyhow," she added, with a flash of resentment, "I am still alive. I have my moments of happiness." Is he still drifting? she asked herself, and could find no answer. He has not lost his old gaze of an aimless fanatic . . . Of a fanatic with inspiration, but without vision.

"Why did you run away?" he asked. "I mean, really."

There was a long hesitation; then she replied in a controlled voice, "I don't know. I suppose I was trying to make over my life."

"And you failed."

"Yes, yes, I failed. But I am not finished. I am still going on."

"You tried to break away, but you couldn't. You had to fall back on the things that had hurt you."

Her smile was defiant. "If only I had kept my health. I had not counted on illness. That was something outside. It had nothing to do with my real self."

"How did it begin? I mean, this cough you are doing your best to hide?"

"I can't remember. There were so many beginnings. I went

to work too soon after pneumonia. Then it came back, the pneumonia, twice, in six months. That used up all I had saved, and I had to start to work before I was well . . . because . . . oh, well, because . . ."

"Yes, I know." His tone had softened, and she thought: This is Craig as I knew him. He is just as he used to be.

"And then, what?" he asked suddenly, still looking away from her.

"The only job I could get was in a basement. I stayed there till I began to spit blood . . . just once . . . and then . . . and then . . . Well, the doctor said I had to stop and go to this place in the Adirondacks."

"You ought to have gone," Craig said, with a savage pity in his changed voice. "You ought to have gone at once. You may have waited too long."

"No, it isn't so bad. He—the doctor thinks I shall be well again. What I need most is plenty to eat." She laughed, but the high flush still reddened her face. "Anyhow, I couldn't leave Timothy. I couldn't leave him with nobody to look after him. If you could have seen those children in cheap homes . . . Oh, no, I couldn't go away till Timothy was . . . was . . ."

"Your mother will look after him."

"Not unless Father comes back. That's why I am here."

"You haven't asked him?"

"Not yet, I'm waiting till I see him."

Craig looked doubtful. "There's a war on, you know, and a farm. He is the mainstay of this place. Mrs. Oliver and your father together do most of the work. Can you stop thinking of yourself long enough to understand what it means to see the crops you've sweated over waste away and die for lack of people to gather them?"

"You're here, aren't you?"

"I am going next week."

She sighed, but her voice was still hopeful. "I know. Oh, I do know, but, after all, I am his child. Haven't I always meant more than anything else?"

"What about Mrs. Fitzroy? She is well-off, and she has nothing to worry over but the war and the Red Cross."

"She doesn't like children. I don't mean she isn't kind. Aunt Charlotte has always been kind. She will do anything for me but take Timothy to live with her. That is natural, I suppose. She wants to live in her own way."

Craig chuckled. "Well, that sounds modern. It even sounds like us." He looked straight into Roy's unfaltering eyes. "Roy, why did you do it?"

A tremor quivered through Roy's features, and was gone in an instant. "I don't know, Craig."

"Will you stop saying you don't know. To please me, will you stop saying that?"

"But I don't. Honestly, I don't know."

"Well, stop saying it." His voice was tense with annoyance.

"Sometimes," Roy said, "I think I was not myself. Then, I think I was myself, only more so."

Craig was scowling again. "Oh, all right, all right."

Timothy stirred restlessly, and Roy lowered him to the floor of the car. "Shall we go on, Craig? Or might he play about the roots of that cedar?"

"We'll let him out for a bit. I suppose he won't run away?"

She smiled proudly. "He wouldn't leave me. If I give him a few sticks, he will be perfectly quiet. I think he is a born architect, because he is never tired of building things." She watched Craig lift Timothy to the ground, and then her glance followed the child's sober trot to the roots of a dying cedar. "Here, darling, I'll help you find something to play with." Jumping out of the car, she raked together some twigs and bits of bark, and spread them out in front of the small, outstretched hands. Then, as Timothy fell eagerly to work, she turned and sank down on the running board.

"Haven't you anything to stop that cough, Roy?"

She nodded, holding her thin chest. "I have, but I didn't bring it," she answered presently. "But this will stop in a minute. It isn't always so bad."

"You must do something about it. You can't put it off."

"Oh, I shall be all right, as soon as I know what will happen to Timothy." After a sharp spasm, the cough died down, and she spoke in a natural voice, "The doctor has arranged everything."

Leaning against the side of the car, Craig gazed over her head, toward the slow-cropping sheep. "I can't understand Mrs. Fitzroy. You would think a child like that would be just what she needed to fill her life."

Roy laughed. "She prefers it empty. Some people do." After a pause, she continued on the same flippant note: "You can't blame her, Craig. Uncle William must have made full measure and brimming over."

Craig had turned and was gazing, in a kind of fascinated incredulity, at Timothy. Completely absorbed, the child was playing with his bits of bark and twigs under the cedar.

"He will keep that up for an hour," Roy said. "It is the easiest thing in the world to amuse him."

"He is a great little chap," Craig said. "I hope his world will be better than ours."

"Oh, it must be. It will be." A subdued thrill ran through Roy's tone. "Doesn't that mean more than anything else? Just for him to have a good world to live in."

Craig shook his head. "He will have to make his own world. Yes, he's worth hoping for, but, somehow—do you know?—I cannot believe in him."

She looked up startled. "You know?"

"Oh, my dear . . . You precious idiot . . . Haven't I seen your face?"

"It was only because of Mother. I promised . . . But I hoped I shouldn't see you."

He smiled, with a gleam of mockery. "Well, no harm is done, yet. I am as safe as this old bus, perhaps safer. But you look as if you had popped out of the wrong end of the telescope. You could scarcely have done worse if you'd stayed properly at home and married me."

"You didn't care, Craig. Not really. What you loved in me was that some other man had made me suffer."

His smile changed to a frown. "I doubt, my dear, whether I am as subtle as all that."

She flung out her hand, as if she were pushing him from her. "Well, we are both free now, and we are glad of it."

"I have to keep free. That is the only way I can do my job, and my job is the chief thing while it lasts. It is a bit odd, isn't it," he said thoughtfully, "the way personal happiness appears to have lost its old stature?"

She nodded. "Yes, I remember the war in Spain. You wanted to go, but something was always pulling you back. I suppose it was happiness-hunting."

"This is like that, yet, in a way, different." He laughed shortly, still frowning. "It's devilish, isn't it, that an obscene act, like war, may release a flash—if only a flash in the pan—of moral idealism?"

"Does it never last?" She looked at Timothy in his play. "It might be thrilling to help build a new world."

His gaze followed hers and rested thoughtfully on the child. "I suppose it might last, the idealism, but it never has. Not long enough, anyhow, to build a better world." After a moment, he asked with sudden bitterness, "Why was it, Roy? Why? Why? My God, what a muddle you made of things!"

"Well, life still goes on, after a muddle."

"Where is the child's father?" He was looking away from her with a wandering yet singularly intent expression.

"I don't know. He may be dead. He went back to England."

"You might at least have written."

"I know, Craig . . . but what was there for me to say? How could any of them have understood? It all happened the night of the storm. That storm seemed to be everywhere. We talked all night . . . Oh, but I've said this so often!" She broke off, hesitated in perplexity, and began again: "His life, too, was ruined. I suppose," she added quietly "it meant nothing more than two ruined lives coming together . . ."

"What did you know of him? What do you know now?"

She shook her head. "Nothing. Only that he was born in Canterbury, and he was more unhappy than I was. I do not know even so much as his name. He would have looked for me if he had known mine . . . I did not wish him to find me . . . It was over . . ."

"My God!" Craig exclaimed furiously. "It sounds mad. It sounds fantastic. You are telling me this, and yet you cannot make me believe it."

"Sometimes I don't believe it myself."

"You were always the sort . . . I knew this much . . . to be betrayed by your good impulses."

"Good or bad. When we are desperate, we sometimes act outside ourselves. Or it may be only that our real self breaks out."

Craig was silent while he watched her. Does he hate me? Roy asked herself. Was it ever love that he felt? Was I ever more to him than a mistaken adventure?

He looked slowly away, and then back again. "But you were not like that, Roy?"

"I must have been like that. I don't know why it happened. I know it did happen."

"You said he was unhappy." The thought of that unknown man, she could see, was still harassing him. "You were sorry for him, but that isn't enough."

Her spirit flared up, and she made an effort to speak honestly, and without pathos. "That was part of it. I told you he was desperate. I felt pity for him, but it was not pity alone. There was something else. I wanted to trample on something. I wanted to hurt, because I had been hurt so . . . so deeply. I wanted to end everything I had known, and to begin again differently . . . oh, so differently that I could not ever, ever, ever come back."

"But you did come back," he repeated, with stubborn truth.

Her face twitched. "Not to myself. There are more than three years between what I was then and what I am now."

"You had a ghastly time. I know that. With less pride and more sense, you might have been spared the worst of it."

"Still, I came through. I haven't given up yet, and I have Timothy."

"Yes, I know, Timothy." He bit back his words sharply, and began over again. "I rather like that chap Timothy. He is the symbol of something . . . the unknown future, I suppose . . . But why did you name him Timothy? Whatever the future becomes, it isn't likely to be Godfearing."

"I didn't think, or I didn't care." There was scorn in her flippancy. "It wasn't a family name."

"Will you let me help him, Roy? Will you let me help you and the child?"

She flinched. "Do you think you can pity me?"

"I shouldn't dare." His levity had returned. "That's your trouble with any man. You are too strong to be pitied. All I meant was, I have more than I need, and you have less. My father died last year, you know—or don't know."

"I had not heard. But I do not need that kind of help any longer. Aunt Charlotte offers me money. So does Mother. What I really need is somebody to love Timothy until I am well again. I have to get well as fast as I can. I cannot die and leave him, not even with Father."

"What will you tell him? Your Father, I mean."

"The truth. Father can stand the truth, always."

Craig was watching her lips. "Yes. Yes, I suppose so. I was wondering."

"You don't think Mrs. Oliver has changed him?" She frowned anxiously.

"I am not sure. She does change people."

"How does she?" There was a cutting edge to Roy's tone.

"It isn't what she does." Craig was seeking the right word. "You can't see her, day in and day out, without feeling her strength, and . . . yes, her wisdom. And she is entirely free." He hesitated, scowling slightly. "There are no strings to her life."

"Did she change you?"

"I don't know. Something or somebody did. It may have been the river, or just living out-of-doors, in the country. I was all in, when I came here last year. Now I'm fit for killing, if I ever shall be." He held out his arms to the child. "Come on, Timmy. Playtime is over."

Timothy looked regretfully at his hut of bark, walled in by a border of small stones. "Bye, bye," he said, and scrambled up from the ground.

"Is she attractive?" Roy was asking.

"Attractive?" Craig echoed derisively. "I can't tell you. I've never thought much about it."

"She must be well over fifty. Craig, he can't be in love with her."

"I don't know. I haven't thought. Somehow, love isn't all that it used to be."

"You mean . . ."

"I mean, there's something else. There is something bigger than one person—or than two persons."

"I suppose it's the war," Roy said. She stretched out her hand. "Come, Timmy."

But Craig was still holding out his arms, and Timmy dropped his last piece of twig and trotted over to him.

"You see." Craig turned a casual smile on her, as he lifted the child into the car. "Babies instinctively prefer the stronger."

"Yes, he likes you." Roy appeared happy about it. "Usually, he is shy with strangers. Drive through," she added. "I'll shut the gate after you."

A moment later, while she settled herself in the front seat and took Timothy in her lap, she looked beyond the screen of cedars to the spirals of thin blue smoke that curled over the burning leaves. "I wonder," she said, in a distant tone, "what it can be about Mrs. Oliver."

# II

SUDDEN light shone through the trees. Ahead of them, they saw a low house of weathered brick, with a square Georgian porch, overhung by a microphylla rose-bush, on which a few sad, pale, imperfect October roses were still blooming.

"Somebody is singing!" Roy said, as a mournful voice, charged with the deep vibrations of autumn, floated to them from beneath the elms on the lawn.

"That's Blind Dick, with his hound Rambler. He is weeding the grass, and he always sings at his work."

"Is he blind?"

"He has been blind for years. Nobody knows how old he is, but, before Mrs. Oliver trained him to weed the flowerbeds, he and his hound used to go about the country looking like scarecrows. Now, he draws his wages every week, with the rest of the hands, and he lives in a cabin on the other side of the peanut-fields."

"Does he earn his living?" Roy asked, peering under the elms.

"There isn't a better hand on the farm. He can tell any weed from a flower by the feel of it."

As they drew nearer, the singing voice rose and fell, and rose again from the shadows.

*"Let the wind blow east, let the wind blow west,*
*O Lawd, I don' wanter die in a s-t-o-r-m."*

"He doesn't sound blind," Roy said.

"To watch him at work, you'd never know it. He sees with his fingers."

78

"Are there others?"

"He is the only blind one. But she has several disabled farmhands. She is doing things like that all the time, not giving charity so much as helping misfits to help themselves. Your father tells her she is one alone against Nature. Her husband was like her, they say, only more so. They never turned off a man or a dog without help."

Roy glanced at him quickly. "Mother doesn't like her."

"She wouldn't," Craig assented tolerantly. "They belong to different worlds, for one thing. Your mother is a last surviving great lady. Even her chronic invalidism stems from a dying order."

"I know. When she wasn't able to face poverty, she fell ill. Yet she isn't weak," Roy added hastily. "In many ways, Mother is the strongest of us all. She always wins the last battle."

He looked at her closely. "You never really cared for her."

"It is a queer thing to say, but I used to imagine, as a little child, that I was a changeling. I can't remember when I first began to take sides with Father. Nobody was ever fair to him, especially Mother."

"Like other superstitions," Craig replied, with scoffing humour, "filial affection is out of date. But you are right. Nobody was ever fair to your father. Nobody," he added slowly, "but Mrs. Oliver."

"He isn't in love with Mrs. Oliver," Roy insisted. "How can he be?"

Craig laughed. "I don't know. I doubt whether he knows himself. But I wonder when you women will stop magnifying the importance of love. One would think you'd had enough of that kind of trouble . . . There is nobody here, it seems. Shall we get out and walk down to the fields?"

"Where can we find Father?"

"He will be about somewhere. How far can Timothy trot?"

"When he is interested, he forgets to be tired."

Craig had turned the Ford into a grassy track near the garage, and after he had stopped, he picked up the child, swung him high in the air, and set him down in the middle of the path. "Do you want to trot, Timmy?"

"Go," said Timothy.

"He is wide awake now," Roy said, "and he is finding his tongue." Her eyes grew dreamy, while she watched Timothy plunge into the windrow of crisp yellow leaves. The sound delighted him, and he gurgled with merriment, as he kicked through the rustling elm-leaves and crushed them under his feet.

"If only I can keep him as happy as this," Roy murmured, with a quick fall in her voice.

"Well, he looks as if he were born plus. There are but two classes of human beings, after all, the plus and the minus . . . Stop that, youngster!" Craig called out. "Nobody plucks Mrs. Oliver's prize rooster."

"He has never before seen chickens and ducks running loose," Roy said, as she caught the child's arm. "He finds them exciting."

"Oh, he'll learn," Craig's hand slipped from the child's shoulder and grasped Roy's wrist. "Damn your pride," he muttered under his breath.

Suddenly, it seemed to Roy that the hour and the scene, and even the slow rain of leaves, were all charged with surprise. Fear set a pulse in her mind, and a glimmer of light stirred the darkness. Everything that had been dead, or at least sleeping, was alive and awake. But it is over, she told herself. Nothing is so completely over as a fire that has burned out. "My pride is all I have left," she said aloud.

Though Craig's smile was intimate and even tender, there was an accent of mockery in his voice. "Well, I'd be but a poor exchange for your pride."

"Yes, I'll keep my pride, thank you," she tossed back angrily, while her face flushed with resentment.

Below the river front of the house, the almost obliterated terraces fell away to the scalloped edge of the James. Farther down, there were many clusters of willows, gnarled and bent with age, but still veiled in a deep fring of yellow-green, which whitened to silver as the light wind turned the leaves over and back again. When the child stooped to pick the reddish brown flowers sprinkling the grass, Roy caught him up almost impatiently, and hastened on to the small dilapidated house near the water, where she could see her father directing the field-hands.

"Is Father still working?" she asked.

"He is just leaving off. That used to be the overseer's house, but it is now dropping to pieces."

"Does he live there? Why doesn't he have the roof mended?"

"You wouldn't ask if you stayed here. Food comes first. Men work and armies march on their stomachs."

"Does he sleep up at the big house?"

"Where else? There is room for us all."

Her quick pace slackened, and she looked across the grass to the distant stretches of fallow-land, sown thickly with scrub pine and broomsedge. "They let so much land run to waste," she said, withdrawing her gaze.

"Yes, it is a big farm, and they are able to work only a small part of it. All that land is worn out. It would cost too much to reclaim it. After the losses this year, even fewer crops will be planted. As it is, we lost a good half of our hay, though Mrs. Oliver put on overalls and pitched hay with the rest of us."

"She must be strong."

"As an oak. There is no use trying to farm in Virginia, unless you have the endurance of an oak. You have to fight everything, from insects to the elements."

He was giving her time, Roy thought, not ungratefully. He was making idle talk, while he waited for her to stop coughing and recover her breath.

"Fly! Fly! Fly!" Timothy was jumping up and down, while a cloud of larks rose, with a whirring noise, from the powdery bloom of a near meadow. In the midst of the startled flock, a tall upright figure, in blue overalls, moved swiftly, as if it obeyed some natural harmony in earth or air. "That must be Mrs. Oliver," Roy said. "She looks as if she were a part of the autumn."

"She is that," Craig answered, watching the asters and life-ever-lasting divide into a path. "But it is true of her in all seasons. I thought that about her in the spring. Not because she looks young. She isn't youthful. She is elemental."

The tall figure left the meadow and the rising larks, and came over the bright grass under the willows. Slant-wise, by her side, a faintly coloured shadow appeared to flow in ripples, with the light movement of water.

"I thought she was fat," Roy said, in surprise. "But she isn't soft. She is all muscle, bone and muscle."

"You must have seen her before."

"Not for years. Mother always hated to have us come here." Then, as Kate Oliver approached, lifting her firm, weather-beaten face to the sunshine, the girl whispered: "And she looks good. So few strong persons look good."

Craig nodded. "There is an inward beauty that breaks through. I never used to believe in it."

Kate's warm brown eyes were flooded with happiness. "So you have come at last, Roy." She held out her work-roughened hands and gathered the girl into her arms. "What a beautiful child!" she exclaimed the next minute, as she stooped over Timothy.

Through the small yellow leaves sunlight sprinkled her hair, which was gray on the temples and burnished to a pale copper where the short waves curled up from the deeply tanned nape of her neck. When she rose and glanced round again, her smile enveloped the harvested fields, the ragged meadow, and the near and far distance. She loves the land as if it were human, Roy thought. It is life, the whole of life, that she feels. She has learned how life must be lived . . . Aloud, she said, after a pause: "Yes, this is Timothy. Tell the lady your name, darling."

The child looked up with his rare winning smile. "I . . . is."

"You dear!" Kate said, as he reached toward her; and Craig who had watched the meeting, glanced at Roy in surprise. "He has your smile, Roy."

"It is the first time he has smiled since he came. He hated Queenborough, except for the pigeons."

"Doggies! See doggies!" Timothy cried.

Roy followed his pointing hand. "Pat and Percy have found Father down by the river."

"He is waiting for you. Go down to him, Roy. Craig and I have to see a man about peanuts." Before turning away, Kate looked after the girl and the child as they moved over the green terraces toward the rippling edge of the water. "Roy must have been ill," she said, presently.

# III

CRAIG was watching the two figures, with their thin, slanting shadows, one long, one short, flitting beside them. "She is ill now, but she hasn't talked about it —not to me, anyhow. It is a rotten deal," he added, half angrily, "that life so often goes on after it comes a cropper."

Kate sighed. "What would become of the child? I suppose the little boy is her child."

"Yes, you could see that. Mrs. Timberlake is trying not to let it be known. She is willing to help Roy, but she doesn't like having the child about. You can't blame her. She has a tradition to keep up."

"Why did Roy come back?"

A wry smile distorted Craig's pleasant mouth. "Why does anyone ever come back?"

Kate shook her head. "I don't know. I have often wondered. But there are some lives, I suppose, in which the best comes after the worst has happened."

"You are thinking of Asa."

"Well, who could have had a meaner youth . . . or a meaner maturity?" She was looking, through narrowed eyelids, at Asa hurrying to meet his daughter and his grandchild. Had he expected the child? she asked herself, and what would he think of such a return? "But he is happy at last," she continued. "Doesn't he appear happy?" A laugh, gay yet tender, broke from her lips. "He used to say that his suppressed desire was to be a hired man on a farm."

84

"He was dreaming then of a glorified hired man. But he waited a long time."

"What else could he do? When he lost his job, of course he became not a help, but a burden. It is odd, though, that the thing he dreaded most should have set him free in the end."

Craig nodded. "That may be one reason life goes on . . . often happily enough, after failure. Not the fact, if it is a fact, but the hope."

"Yes, he had his hope. And he seized the exact right moment. I mean, the moment when he could save something out of the wreck. Isn't that the true secret of happiness: To recognize your one best moment, and to grasp it before it eludes you?"

"But, Roy, too, saw her moment—or thought she did."

"Was that, for her, the right moment?"

Craig shrugged his lean, slightly stooping shoulders. "Well, they were both riding for a fall, weren't they? They both failed . . ." He checked himself, hesitated, and then finished slowly: "And life goes on."

"Asa's hope has become his dream," Kate said. "He has his work too. Something in him belongs to the earth."

Her deep, wise look swept the fields and the river, and beyond the river, the far level horizon. Watching her, silently, Craig felt, without words, but with a kind of inarticulate insight: Her nature is rooted in some hidden identity with the land. She has the gift of creation. Whatever she touches lives and thrives, because of some downward seeking and upward springing vitality in her own spirit . . . I can think these things, though I can't say them, he told himself, not aloud, anyhow. I may be mentally unbridled, but I am emotionally tonguetied. I . . . oh, hell and the devil, does it make any difference?

"There is something—a sort of happiness—in the air," he said presently.

Kate laughed, with her quick humour. "In spite of grasshoppers and caterpillars and potato-bugs and wheat-worms and Japanese beetles and Mexican beetles . . . oh, and blight and drought and a drawn battle with the four seasons . . . But I forget all these things, even the insect war, when I see Asa's face. Then I tell myself the end may yet be easier than the beginning."

"If that will last," Craig said, weighing each separate word. "If only Roy's visit does not begin to make trouble."

"To make trouble?" She threw a startled glance at him.

"I mean, and you know, that Roy may persuade him to go back to Lavinia."

"But she couldn't. Why, I thought she was devoted to him." Indignation pulsed in her usually serene voice.

"She is devoted to him, but there is the child. The child makes all the difference."

"Still, Lavinia . . . You know, as well as I do, what sort of marriage that was."

"I know. But it isn't so much a marriage with Lavinia as a convention. She wants him back, because of what people are saying. It mortifies her pride to appear as a deserted wife." He laughed, and continued more lightly. "I've always got on well with Mrs. Timberlake, first as Stanley's lover, and then as Roy's. I fancy it was because I treated her less as a woman than as a problem. Oddly enough, that seemed to flatter her moral vanity."

"Think of the work Asa is doing here." Kate spoke as if she had not listened to what he was saying. "Nobody could take his place. He works from before daybreak till long after dark, and he is raising food the country needs and must have. Of course, one man with little help cannot do things in a big way, but, all the same, he is doing big things. I cannot believe he would fall out."

Craig frowned. "You are right. I know you are right . . . but Lavinia doesn't see it like this. Queenborough—at least the Queenborough of her generation upholds her. After all, I imagine, she is a bitter-ender."

"Roy isn't like that. Have you forgotten how Roy was about Peter? She let him go, without lifting her little finger."

"I haven't forgotten." His lips, not his eyes were smiling. "And I haven't forgotten, either, that she let me go, without lifting her little finger. But she is thinking, now, of the child."

"Doesn't anybody think of the farm?"

Craig shook his head. "You and Asa may. What Lavinia thinks, and what she has probably told Roy, is that you, my dear . . . Oh, well, you know what she thinks and what she says."

There was an edge of exasperation in Kate's retort. "She is saying, and no doubt thinking, that, at our safe and sober age, we are using the farm as an excuse for living in sin."

Craig chuckled. "Or living in sin as an excuse for the farm. Doesn't sin always come first?"

What energy of mind and heart, Craig thought, as he followed her in the direction of Blind Dick's singing voice. Under the elms, he could see the old Negro's kneeling figure, and stretched out on the grass, the smooth black and brown body of the hound Rambler. No one but Kate could have helped there, in that simple goodness which was the only infallible way. But what is simple goodness, he questioned, except character which has overflowed from its source, which upholds both the visible and the invisible world? You must pass through hell, as I did, to learn that, he told himself, but when you have learned this truth, in the hard way, it will stay by you as long as you have need of it.

As Blind Dick felt their approach, he raised his head and poured out his voice, until the hymn rose and trembled, and swelled triumphantly, as if it were tossed away on a rising wind. Negroes singing at their work was one of Craig's earliest impressions of Hunter's Fare. Do they sing because they are happy or unhappy, he had always wondered.

> *O Lawd, I'se a-comin' home,*
> *O Lawd, I'se a-comin' home,*
> *Open wide de gates, O Lawd,*
> *    I'se a-comin' home.*

# IV

O H, BUT Father, Roy thought. Will Father be changed?

Her pace slackened, while the child fell out of step, and she looked anxiously, beyond the sunken terraces, toward the river, which was changing from blue to silver as light rippled, like wind, over its surface. Unmown grass ran down to the water's edge, and farther away, on the right, a sad little path, barely more than an impression, twisted, among the trunks of the willows, to the brick building where Asa now had his office.

No wonder she loves it, Roy said to herself, touched by some native spirit or poetry of place. This is her past . . . yet she does not stay in the past. I suppose that is why people, like Mother, who belong to the past, will always misjudge her. Timothy stumbled, and after helping him to his feet, Roy waited for him to pluck with clumsy hands a few of the brown daisies.

"This is James River, Timothy. Say it after me: James River."

"Wiver," Timothy repeated obediently. "Birdies . . . Doggies . . . Flovers . . ." How good he is, and how happy, she told herself. I wonder if he will remember this afternoon all his life. Or is he too young for memory?

At the end of the twisted path, before a half-buried stone door-step, her father was waving to her. Then as she moved toward him, he left the group of field-hands and came to meet her, with Pat and Percy bounding ahead. Like a shadow falling, anxiety clouded her face. What had her desertion done to him?

89

What had Mrs. Oliver done to him? Had his unselfishness or his endurance broken at last?

She saw him lift his hand, and let it fall slowly. She saw the light on the rippling water behind him. She saw the fringed curtain of the willows divide and drop together again over the shallow path. Then, as he came nearer, she heard his welcome and met the eager love in his face. But he is different, she thought. Something has changed him. It was not only that he looked weather-beaten and sunburned and healthy from work in the fields. The change went farther and deeper. He looked as if he had been to the end of his life, and had come out again somewhere else, in another beginning.

"Roy! My darling child, Roy!"

"Daddy. Oh, Daddy, Daddy!" As the childish name burst from her lips, a frozen surface in her mind broke up and the fragments melted to tenderness. For three years, she had not dared to use that name in her thoughts.

He opened his arms, and she clung to him, still holding Timothy by the hand. "Oh, but Daddy, I've wanted you. I know you will help me."

The old quizzical smile, mocking yet tender, brightened his eyes. "So you didn't come back till you needed me."

"I've needed you all the time. You will never know—never—never—never, Daddy. I was ashamed to give up till I couldn't go on any longer. I've been terribly ill. I am ill now. Can't you see?"

His look dwelt on her. "I can see . . . And this is the little boy?"

"Oh, you know. You must know . . ." There was wildness in her voice. "Aunt Charlotte was trying to spare Mother. Mother feels it so dreadfully. She made me promise not to . . . not to . . . But he is mine, Daddy, and I want him. I do want him."

"Well, he's a fine little chap." Asa was leaning down to the child, who gave him one tight fist stuffed full of crushed flowers.

"I is," he said, without waiting for the silly question that grown-ups never learned to answer for themselves. "Wiver. Birdics. Doggies."

"He looks bright." Why did everybody say that? Then after a brief silence, "Is he Craig's son, Roy?"

"No. Oh, no, no."

From his worn face, his eyes, wise with tolerance, regarded her steadfastly. "But he is my grandchild?" His glance wandered to Timothy, who was trying to scramble up on Pat's shoulders.

"Yes. Yes, he is your grandchild."

"Well, he is a splendid boy. Tell me about his father, my dear. But only tell me as much or as little as you wish me to know . . ." Though he spoke so quietly, there was a stricken look in his eyes.

Roy's face quivered, and for an instant she swallowed hard, as if she were going to burst into tears. Then, with an effort, she controlled her voice and answered in an expressionless tone: "You remember the night of the storm. It was the night when you looked for me. I ran out, and you followed me . . . and looked for me."

"Yes. Yes, I remember. It was the end of August. That was a bad August."

"I went out in the rain, because I wanted never to come back. I hated everything, even you. I hated you because . . . oh, because I had loved you . . . but most of all I hated Craig . . . I wanted to hurt him. There was the rain. I walked till I couldn't go on . . . Then I met him. Timothy's father . . . and he took me home with him. He was staying in a borrowed flat, all alone. And he was worse off than I was. That drew me to him. He was the only person who seemed more unhappy than I was . . ."

"Yes, my child. Yes, I know."

"He was going to England. He was born in Canterbury. War was coming, he felt, and he wanted to be in it, so he wouldn't . . . he wouldn't feel shut out and alone any longer. We were both at the end of things. Our lives were ruined . . . That is all I know," she finished helplessly. "I have said it over and over. That is all I know. There isn't anything else . . . Only Aunt Charlotte and Craig will not believe it. They kept asking me to tell them more and more . . . They wouldn't believe that was all. I left at daybreak. The rain was over. Everything was flat and drab and wet and miserable . . . And I was sorry. But I thought it was over. I thought I should never have to tell anyone, or even think of it again. I thought I could put it out of my life . . . Then I went home and found you. Don't you remember?"

"Yes, my dear. Yes, I remember."

"Of course, I didn't know about Timothy. Later, when I found out about Timothy, I went away, and I let nobody know. I went away to New York. I thought I could make my life, but I failed . . ." She broke into low weeping, and he put his arms about her, and drew her close to his heart.

"And you never saw him again? I mean, Timothy's father."

"I couldn't. I didn't even know his name. He was sailing for England. He may be dead now. That was what he wanted . . . just to be killed . . . Oh, but Daddy, why won't Aunt Charlotte and Craig believe there isn't anything more?"

"I don't know, darling. I suppose, it is hard to believe that." He patted her bowed head. "And you named the child Timothy?"

"Yes, Timothy. I always liked Timothy . . . and oh, well, it was different . . . but there isn't anything more, Daddy . . . There was never anything more."

With his arm about her shoulders, he drew her to a bench under a willow. "Sit down, daughter. You look as if you would give way. You don't have to tell me anything. I can see you have been ill."

"But Timothy . . . Is he safe? The river is so near."

"He's safe. We'll keep an eye on him." He disengaged the small arms from the neck of the bored and anxious Pat. "Come with Grandfather, Timothy."

"Grandfaver," Timothy repeated obediently. "Play, Grandfaver."

"Give him some sticks," Roy said.

"Let him find them for himself." Asa led the child to the bench, and showed him a broken branch on the ground. "There's your play, Timmy."

"He knows how." Roy's eyes did not leave the child for an instant. "I had to go back to work when he was only two months old. As he grew older, he learned to lie quiet, and to play with his rattle and rubber toys, while Mrs. Camper, the woman I left him with, sewed on her machine. She was kind-hearted, but she could not afford to give up her dressmaking."

"Was he fed on a bottle?"

"Not at first. I got a job in a basement nearby, on Lexington Avenue. Then I could slip out and come back to him. But I didn't have the right things to eat. I fell ill, and it made him sick too. Then the doctor put him on baby food."

"Poor child." Asa's voice trembled. "I mean you, darling, not Timothy. You were a brave girl."

She laughed, on the edge of tears. "I am not a girl any longer. I'll never feel young . . . except," she added, "in moments."

For the first time, while she glanced away from Timothy, and then quickly back again, she caught a glimpse of her father's puzzled and wondering look. "Well, twenty-six doesn't seem a great age to sixty-three. But you are a brave woman, my dear."

"I knew I had lost, Daddy. That is why I did not come back before. I hated to come home a failure . . . and, then, I knew, too, that Mother would feel so . . . so terribly."

"Well, none of us has been a success, my dear. Not when you look at us on the outside, and that is the only way the world ever sees us. If we measure results by appearances. There isn't one of us, not even Kate, who could be called a shining mark. Yet some of us," he was smiling now, "manage to do pretty well in the end."

Roy laughed. "Craig will tell you . . ." She broke off and asked: "Is he still telling you the same things?"

Asa chuckled. "Yes. Yes, I suppose so. Only his forgotten man used to be next door. Now he lives on the other side of the world."

"But, still, Craig remembers?" There was a deeper note in her voice.

"Oh he remembers." Her father's eyes were grave. "Craig remembers everything in his heart."

"In his heart," she repeated, without emphasis, and appeared to dismiss the thought of Craig from her mind. "But you, Daddy . . . You look quiet and happy, as if you had found something to brood over. When you came up the path, just now, I felt a stillness about you . . ."

Yes, it was true, she told herself, as her glance wavered from the child at her feet. Asa's face wore that look of inward stillness after conflict which comes to those who have fought their way through the dark forest. The peace in his faintly ironic gaze was the resignation of defeat that has been turned into victory. He has what he has always most wanted, she thought, with clear-eyed penetration, even if it seems but a little thing to everyone else. But how could she ask him, in the face of his hard-won serenity, to give up the first and the last happiness he had ever known?

"Your future is still there," he was saying. "You may even find love again. Love has a way of springing up in bare places."

She shook her head. "After you've gone hungry, love isn't everything."

"Well, whatever happens, there is Timothy. Timothy isn't to blame because he came when he did. He is the child of the unknown, and the sky is the boundary for the unknown. Did you ever think of it that way, my dear? You may build your life on the unknown, but not on a mistake. After all, he has Canterbury in his blood. He may even have a cathedral. That's a good enough corner-stone for a life." There was a whimsical overtone in his serious voice.

Her smile answered his. "I try to feel that way. Some mistakes are worth paying for . . . And isn't he beautiful?"

"He is a nice child. I oughtn't to say it, but, already, he is a bit nearer to me than Andrew's boys—or than Andrew. There was always something a trifle too superior about Andrew. He is my son, but he never forgets that his father was a successful failure."

"Oh, I'm glad. I mean, I'm glad you feel like that about Timothy. Then, perhaps—" she hesitated and stammered slightly—"perhaps you won't mind so . . . so dreadfully. . . ."

"Mind, Roy?"

"I mean, mind going back. . . ."

"Going back?"

"Going back home . . ." Meeting his startled look, she added hurriedly: "I forgot . . . I've told Craig, but I haven't told you about Mother."

"No." His voice was grave. "You haven't told me."

Watching him, she thought: It is harder than I knew it would be. There was a strangely remote quality in his expression, not only in his withdrawn gaze, but in the smooth, tanned planes of his face, which grief had fined down to a hidden core of integrity. He looked sensitive yet, in a way, hard and unbreakable.

"No, you haven't told me," he repeated. And as he smiled at her, she knew why she had come to him, why she was depending upon him. All the others had gone down into that thick darkness of failure, of what the past was and was not, of what time was and was not. He, alone among them, had put the darkness aside. He had come out again into the future, into the shape of things that were still becoming.

"You haven't told me," he said again, for the third time, waiting, patient and detached, for her answer.

"I forgot," she heard herself saying over and over. "I forgot." Then, breathing quickly, she stumbled on, with her head down and her eyes fixed on the child. "You can see how it is. Can't you see, Daddy?"

"Yes, I can see. You are not yourself. You look," he said slowly, "as if you had been ground down to powder."

Her glance, bright with watchfulness, flew to the trees, to the clouds, and then back to Timothy. "No, darling, don't go so far away. Stay close by Grandfather," she said, and went on again, in a strangled voice, keeping her cough well under control: "The doctor thinks I can be cured. He wants me to go to this place in the Adirondacks—a kind of camp, where I may live out of doors. He has already arranged for me to be taken. But I couldn't leave Timothy. I didn't tell him—the doctor, I mean —that I was coming to Queenborough. I thought I could stay one night, and then go straight back to New York. They expect me day after tomorrow . . ."

"You must go, Roy. You must go day after tomorrow."

"But I couldn't leave Timothy . . . not with strangers to look after him. You see, I thought you were still at home . . . I didn't know . . . I didn't know you had gone away.

Then I found Aunt Charlotte. Mother had had a heart attack —not a bad one—and Aunt Charlotte had spent the night with her . . . It was Aunt Charlotte who told me about you."

"Did you see your mother?" His tone was distant and oddly flattened.

"For a little while. She was not glad to have me come. She always loved Stanley best . . . And now she feels . . . oh, terribly . . . She pretended to the nurse that Timothy belonged to somebody else—to some refugee."

Asa nodded. "Well, that isn't hard to understand, is it?"

"No, that isn't hard. I could see how she felt. She told me she would help me as much as she could—I mean, with money—but she would not acknowledge that Timothy had any claim on her." Her eyes gazed at him defiantly. "Were all the people of her generation like that?"

"All I ever knew, my dear. And many of your own generation are like that. After all, you must remember, it was your own doing."

"I do remember. And she feels as bitterly about you Daddy. She thinks you deserted her."

"I suppose she does, Roy. I have never expected anything else. In a way, I can admire her for standing so loyally by her guns."

"You did desert her, didn't you, Daddy?"

"That's one way of looking at it." There was a gleam of resentment in his steady eyes. "That is the Queenborough way, no doubt, and it is the outside way. But you know what my life was in that house."

"Oh, I know, Daddy. How could I help knowing? You never had anything."

"I had something," he said, slowly. "I had those stolen Sunday afternoons, now and then, down here on the farm."

"But that was so little."

"It was more than you know. It made me able to bear the rest of—of a mean life. When I could stand it no longer at home, I could break away for a few hours, not more than once or twice a month, and come down to be out of doors—your mother hated the country—with Kate and the dogs. That would pick me up, and give me the courage—or the desperation—to go on again, from the house to the factory and, back again, from the factory to the house. It was a round of purgatory. I hated both places, the house and the factory."

"You never told us. You never blamed us."

"It wasn't your fault. We are as we are. Till I lost my job, I had to stick by it. What else could I do? Your mother needed my salary, small as it was. But, when your Uncle William died, and I lost my job, I became only a burden." Again that grim smile was bitten in, as if with acid, about his mouth. "I saw that. Your mother did not mind letting me see it. And that helped. I began to think. I even began to tell myself it wasn't too late to save something out of the wreck. That, I believe, was your doing. I should have stayed with you as long as you needed me. When you went away like that . . . well, I knew that the breakingpoint had come, and I began to think again, not of you, but of saving my own soul alive . . ."

Roy was sobbing. "I was cruel. I was cruel, because I was so . . . so frightened."

"I know. Fear does make us cruel. But I didn't know then. I didn't know you were ever afraid of me."

"Not of you. Never of you, Daddy."

"Well, you hurt me, darling, but you gave me courage. You gave me back my life. There comes a time when a man—any man—must either break away or drop dead in his harness. But for Kate, I should have dropped dead, after you left me. I mean dead in spirit."

"Mother thought you had all you wanted—at least, she thought that till—till Mrs. Oliver . . ."

"No, she knew I wasn't happy, but she had to think that I was. She has the faculty of believing what she knows is not true. You couldn't blame her. She is obliged to delude herself, or she couldn't live nobly."

Though he spoke now, without bitterness, the flicker of that ironic gleam still brightened his look. "I waited long for my time, daughter."

"You waited, but when the time came, you knew it. You did not let it slip by you."

"Yes, I knew my hour. I heard it strike. I knew that, for me, it would not strike again."

"Dear Daddy." She put her lips to his earth-stained hand. "I am glad it was not too late. I am glad you are happy. You are happy, aren't you?"

He patted her head. "Not so you'd know it, Roy, but it suits me. You won't believe me, when I tell you that the best of life doesn't come till you're past sixty. There isn't any of your running wild-fire, perhaps, but, if you prefer a steady glow that doesn't singe, the latter years are the happiest, after you've once learned how to live them." His amused eyes searched her face. "And I owe it all, or most of it, to Kate and the farm. Kate is the sort who can make a starved thing put out and live . . ."

"She is good," Roy said. "I know she is good. You feel goodness about her."

"Yes, she has the right touch." He raised his hand to push aside a branch of the willow, and she saw his face under the trembling shadows of leaves. "I was a misfit, and she showed me where and how I am necessary. I am doing the work I always wanted to do. I am living the sort of life I always wanted to live. If you aren't afraid of the word, I suppose you might call it happiness."

But it is only friendship between them, Roy told herself. How can it be anything else? Mrs. Oliver is wonderful, but she is not the kind of woman a man loves in that way. She is middle-aged now, and even when she was young, she could not have been beautiful. Her husband, of course, must have loved her. She had twenty years of joy in life, she told Aunt Charlotte, and the rest of bare existence was not too much to pay for it. Why? Why? Roy asked. What was there about her? And Aunt Charlotte had smiled her taunting smile of secret wisdom: "Well, for one thing, she is heartening to live with. When things are at their worst, she doesn't sit down and wring her hands or run round in a circle. She insists there's a way somewhere, and looking will find it."

Timothy had come closer, and was reaching up for her arms. When she lifted him to the bench, he cuddled against her, and murmured, "Ti'ed. Timmy's ti'ed."

"Yes, darling. We'll go up to the house, and we'll have a glass of milk from a nice moo-cow." Her eyes rested on him in delight, and she thought: I'd do anything for him. Anything in the world.

She started to speak; then checked herself, while she gazed beyond the deepening lustre on the river to the powdery haze over the distant blue reaches. Downstream, over the yellowing grass on the marshes, there was a sudden flash of wings, and then the slow rhythm and pause of ducks rising.

"Mother wants you to come back to her . . ." The words sounded hollow and false to Roy as she uttered them.

Asa's features were rigid with astonishment—or was it aversion? "Your mother," he repeated slowly, "wishes me to come back to her?"

"If you will come back, I may leave Timothy there—till— oh, till I am well again. If you don't, she says she will have to put him in some—some good home for refugees." Her voice broke. "Mrs. Littlepage has something to do with a home . . ."

"She can't mean it, Roy. Mrs. Fitzroy told me this morning

that your mother is happier now than she has ever been." His mouth twitched, but she could not tell whether it was from amusement or anger. "She—I mean your Aunt Charlotte—says Lavinia is happily wedded to a grievance."

"I know. She feels important and she likes it, because people are making a fuss over her. Aunt Charlotte told me that Mrs. Littlepage, and other women, too, are making a cause of it . . . I mean, of your—your . . ."

"Don't hesitate to say it, Roy. My skin, if not my mind, is tough."

"But she does want you back, Daddy. Her pride wants you back."

He chuckled. "I suppose she thinks she might have me, and keep her grievance. That would be catching two fish with one hook . . . Not, my dear, that it is exactly a laughing matter."

"It isn't, Daddy. Oh, it isn't. How can you laugh?"

"That, my child, is the test of civilized man. The barbarian mind is the serious mind . . . But, of course, you must go to your camp. You must get well. Nothing, not even a war, must come in the way of that."

"You mean?" She looked up, hopefully, from under drenched eye-lashes.

"That I'll go back? Never! Wild oxen couldn't drag me back again. But somehow, in some way, Timothy shall be looked after."

"Oh, but Daddy . . ."

"Don't ask me how. I haven't thought. You must let me think."

"If you can't help me, what will become of us, Daddy?"

"It will be all right, my child," Asa answered soothingly. At the tone of his quiet voice, there flashed back to her a vivid recollection of the time, so long ago, when they were isolated together, and of her father's voice saying over and over: "It will be all right, daughter. It will be all right in a little while . . ."

"I can't see you just as a farmer, Daddy," she said presently. "I can't think of you as anybody's overseer." Leaning nearer, she brushed a lump of clay from the shoulder-straps of his overalls.

"It looks natural enough to me, darling. My heart was always in the earth. It didn't take me long to feel at home in blue denim."

"And yet you married Mother, who hates a farm and everything about it."

"Yes, things happened that way. I suppose I didn't think until afterwards. That's the odd thing about marriage. It may make or spoil a man's life, and yet he reasons less about it than he does about buying a new suit of clothes."

Yes, her marriage with Peter had been like that, Roy remembered. She was so dazed with love that all her other faculties were stunned by the ecstasy, and she had waited to think about it till long afterwards. Then Peter had failed her, and, where love had been, there was only an ache, a wanting, an unsatisfied hollowness . . . But with Craig, she had begun to think before she loved. She had thought of a perfect companionship. She had thought of happiness built upward from a strong basis of reality, of indestructible substance. She had believed this feeling would last, because it was right and true and solid, and invulnerable to change. But Craig, too, had failed her . . . Or, perhaps, she, Roy, had failed Craig and Peter and, in the end, life itself. Was there some flaw in her own nature, she asked now, as she had asked in the past, that made her unequal, or even hostile, to love and to happiness? Pushing the thought away, she said, with absent-minded affection, "You look so different, Daddy. You aren't anxious any longer."

"Not over little ends. I've set my heart on a bigger job. It isn't easy to put the idea into a word, but personal matters, good or bad, have grown smaller. They don't stand out as they used to do . . . I am not sure this isn't a general feeling in wartime."

Roy tried to speak cheerfully but there was a wistful note in her voice. "It would be selfish of me to ask you to go back. I know that, Daddy."

That faint, withdrawn smile closed over his features, as if a blind were dropped suddenly. "I will do what I can, my dear, but my job, now, is to plant and harvest next year's crops."

"Is there nobody to take your place? Do you mean no one, really?"

"Nobody. Not for my place. I work for love of it, and so does Kate. We begin before daybreak, and keep it up till long after dark. We have a few hired men, but not one of them would work for love of the earth and what it gives. Most of them are too old and infirm, or too witless, to earn high wages in the defense plants. Kate and I have to feed and water the horses and cows, and sometimes the hogs and the fowls, too, to make sure they are not being neglected. We haven't taken a day or even an afternoon off since the war began." He bent down and scraped up a clod of soil, with the roots of grass and weeds still matted in the broken earth. For an instant, he looked at the patch of turf through the eyes of a lover. Then, without disturbing Timothy, he carefully settled the scrap back into the torn spot, and smoothed down the edges.

"You see," he said, quietly, "why I can't ask Kate to take on anything else?"

"Yes, I see, Daddy. I see it wouldn't be fair." It was no use, she told herself. Nothing could have spoken more plainly than his tender handling of that fragment of earth. "Oh, but, Daddy, I'm glad! You're right not to change your life. You must not worry about me . . . or about Timothy."

His tired eyes warmed while he looked at her. "It will be all right, darling. Somehow, in some way, we will make Timothy happy." He rose from the bench and glanced up the green terraces to the house at the top. "Craig is looking for you."

"Aren't you coming, too, Daddy?"

"In a few minutes. There's something I must see about in the office. Craig is going to drive the truck to Queenborough late this afternoon, and you and Timothy may ride up with him."

As she moved away with the child, Asa turned back into the path, which looped unevenly round the trunks of the willows.

# V

As Roy went up the long slope, she felt again that start of surprised recognition, of utterly illogical bliss, as if time were running down, and she had walked into another life and another world. Nothing had changed. Circumstances still hedged her round with disaster. Yet, for this one moment, she knew, without knowing how or why, that rightness, truth, sanity, goodness, would prevail in the end. Everything, within and without, was clear and fresh and sparkling: the autumn light, the slow rain of leaves, the recovered harmony in Craig's face, and the vivid stress of impressions spinning airily through her mind.

Craig's head was still damp from a shower, and he had changed into the familiar brown tweed. He is just as I remember him, Roy thought, but aloud she said: "Daddy won't come back, and I believe I am glad. He has found something bigger than I am."

"I knew you'd see that." As she met the altered look in Craig's eyes, she saw her father smiling down on the lump of earth in his hand. Had Craig, also, found something larger than himself, or than anything he had known? Was this what Kate Oliver had made of both their lives, and of her own life as she had lived it, alone, here in this place? I tried, too, to live in my own way, Roy told herself, but it was the wrong way, or it was the wrong way for me. When I fought my hardest to break free from all that had made me what I am, I crashed into failure. But the failure was mine. It was in myself, not in Peter, nor in Craig, nor in Mother, nor in Daddy. It was not in anything outside; it was not in any particular place or time.

While she stood there, looking up into Craig's face, but

holding fast to Timothy's hand, she understood, with a shock of discovery, how much he still meant to her. So there is no escape from anything that is over, she thought; there is no running away from the buried part in one's life. Her voice, when at last she spoke, sounded as faint and far-off as the cry of a bird in the marshes. "So you are going next week?"

"In three days. I leave on Tuesday. But tonight I shall be driving you up to Queenborough. The truck has to go with some machinery." He tossed the child up to his shoulder, and, after a minute's hesitation, walked on beside her. "Up! Up!" Timothy cried, gurgling with pleasure, as he stretched out his arms to the sky.

"I wish you had come sooner," Craig said.

"I didn't come till I had to, Craig." The words rose on a high, sharp note and sank down to a whisper. "Not till there wasn't . . . there wasn't anything else I could do."

He stopped short to let Timothy reach the overhanging branch of a willow. "If you'd had the sense to come sooner, I might have looked after you." His voice quivered with a kind of angry tenderness. It sounded, she thought, bruised.

"No. No. Oh, no, Craig. You don't want that, not really. It is only that you need a forlorn hope." She put out her hand, in an effort to sweep aside the small, shaking leaves and read the truth in his face.

"It is my turn now." He was still frowning. "Last time, you made a muddle of our lives."

She looked away from him to the bright blue distance, which was slowly fading to purple. As the light changed, a solitary black-gum tree near the river blazed out in a flaming torch. "There is colour still left in the world," she said. "Everything looked dead when I came home. But life isn't as drab as it seemed."

"You know you made a mistake, Roy."

"Yes, I know. You don't have to tell me that. I sometimes think everything I ever did was a mistake—or a wrong."

"Marrying Peter was the worst, wasn't it?"

"How can I tell? How could anyone tell? I was happy as long as Peter loved me . . . or I thought he did. But I was too young. We were both too young. Then Stanley came, and Peter wasn't romantic about lost causes."

Craig laughed, as he tossed the child higher under the leaves. "If we were ever lost, Timothy," he said, "we're found again . . . You're going to be well, Roy, and I'm coming home—it may be in a straight-jacket or in a wheel-chair—for you to take care of me. That would be a job after your heart."

"You don't know me, Craig. There are times when my nerves feel like rags on a wire—fluttering rags. Yet there are other times, when—oh, well, when, for a moment, just one moment, I seem to be dancing with joy. Then Timothy and I have the world to ourselves."

She raised her head, drinking in the remembered scents of October, of warm sunshine on earth mould, of burning leaves smothered in smoke, of crushed apples under the old trees in the orchard. "If this could last," she sighed. "I want this one day to go on forever."

With Timothy riding gaily on his shoulder, Craig reached out his free hand, and touched the hollows in her temples, and in her reddened cheeks. "You need somebody to look after you," he said, sternly. "You can't be trusted alone."

She choked, swallowed a sob, and answered defiantly: "Don't dare to be sorry for me."

"How can you stop me? You are going to be well again. In spite of all the foolish things you do, you are too fine to go under. But there's something about you—I don't know what it is—that warns me not to take my hands off you. If I do, you will fly away again and act like an idiot . . ."

A spark of gay derision shone in her eyes. "Well, it won't be your fun, darling!" she said.

"But it's going to be," he retorted, "either my fun or my funeral."

The spark flickered out. "Do you have to be horrid, Craig?" Oh, but it would always be this way, she thought, while she forced herself to look into his guarded eyes. He would never speak in words the one thing she was longing to hear. Always he would compel her to search for hidden meanings, for oblique truths. Nothing could ever become simple and transparent between them. Her effort to make him say, plainly, "I love you" or "I hate you," would bring perpetual defeat.

"Why can't you be simple, Craig? I hate mysteries."

"I am simple, Roy. I am saying in simple words that you need to be taken care of by somebody. And I am saying, too, more simply, if it is possible, that it looks as if the job would have to be mine. If the Navy leaves me hanging about long enough, I shall marry you before I go away. If I am sent off too soon, I mean to marry you with what is left of me when I come home."

Anger burned in her look. "Well, I am not dead—or married to you yet. I shall have something to say about that."

He laughed. "The trouble is that what you say is apt to be wrong. Isn't it too much like what you do?"

"I don't care. We are both free and glad of it. Didn't you say only a few hours ago . . ."

"That was a few hours ago. Time passes. People change." His tone was mocking, ironic, possessive. "Love dies. Duty triumphs."

She shook her head with stubborn resentment. "I suppose . . . oh, I suppose you've never forgiven me. But that's absurd. I don't understand you. I don't even know you."

"You don't have to understand me. Thank God for that! All

you have to do is to look as helpless as you look now, and to feel as you feel now."

"You can't know what I'm feeling."

"I think I can. You aren't as deep as a well, darling."

"And you? What are you feeling about anything? Can't you ever fling back the shutters?"

"You'll have to look through the shutters. Yes, I'm queer, in a way, but I've come to distrust everything that can be put into words. It's as easy to lie as to tell the truth about what we feel."

"If only I could know."

"We can never know. We thought once that we knew, but . . ." He glanced toward the house, and added quickly, "Kate sent me to bring Timothy." Before she could turn away, he put his free arm around her, and drew her into a circle, locked together with the child on his shoulder. As she looked up, startled, he bent down and kissed her lips, at first gently, without passion, and then more roughly, until she felt her breath tremble and fail . . . This is peace, she thought: I have suffered enough. This is the end of strain and violence, and of wanting that is not ever satisfied. The shock of life touched her, and passed on, absorbed by the emptiness and the faint vibration of autumn. As he released her, she glanced round with an air of wild apprehension: "Where is Timothy? Have I lost Timothy?"

"He is here. He is on my other side. And there is Kate looking for us." Swinging the child in his arms, Craig ran on ahead, while Roy followed more slowly. She was still shaken, still bewildered, and she was feeling, without knowing why she felt it, that Timothy had slipped away from her . . . Mrs. Oliver has changed, too. It is like a party, she said to herself, as she went nearer; for Kate was wearing a worn purple-blue cardigan over a fresh blue linen.

After lifting Timothy to the porch, Craig turned back to

Roy, and his arm was about her when he brought her to the door of the house. "You're tired, Roy," he said. "You're all in."

"No, I'm fine. Where has Timothy gone?" Nothing matters, she thought, but Timothy. He is all that I want.

"Mrs. Oliver is going to wash his face and hands. Then she will give him his supper."

"Let me go, too. My face feels as dirty as Timothy's."

"Kate's bedroom is on the first floor. That's the way it was in these old houses. They have bathrooms, but no electricity. Jack put in the showers."

"I thought the place was always hers. Isn't it the Cavendish place?"

"Her family built it before the Revolution. I don't know just when, but they have always owned it. You must have known how it was."

"Oh, I never bothered about it. There are so many of these places on James River. I barely remember the time that I came here. You see, I didn't know about . . . about Father."

As she crossed the porch and entered the wide doorway, Roy's gaze swept the hall to the well of the staircase. "There is a spirit in places," she said. "This house has the feeling of happiness. People who lived here have been happy."

"It isn't the house you feel," Craig answered. "It is Kate. The house alone couldn't create that air. All old houses, I imagine, have some light and some dark moods . . . That room just beyond the staircase is her chamber. It has always been called 'the chamber'."

When Roy opened the door, Timothy ran to meet her, and held up a shining face. Beyond him, there was the old-fashioned chamber, one of the square large rooms on the first floor, with its fishnet canopy over the carved walnut posts of the bed, its soft Brussels carpet, worn thin in spots, but still proudly bearing its faded garlands of roses. In the center of the room, Kate was standing; and as Roy looked into her face, she thought: Craig is right. You can't be with her and not feel what she is. All the lines in her face are lines of unselfishness. They are not disfiguring lines, because they were made by thinking of something larger than any one human being. She looks, Roy thought again, as if she were not afraid of the word, happiness . . . Though there was no questioning in Kate's look, there was warmth and sympathy, and the sense of a strong impersonal identity.

"You must be tired," she said. "You need rest."

"No, only to wash my hands. I feel grimy."

"Well, the bathroom is next door. You will find anything you need in the top drawer of the dressing-table."

"I brought nothing," Roy replied, and added to herself: Not even a lipstick. I haven't had a new lipstick for months, because I was afraid I might need the money for Timothy.

Kate was already at the door, and she turned to glance back, with her hand on Timothy's shoulder. "You're hungry, aren't you, Timmy?" she asked, and the child looked up eagerly, and repeated, "Hung'y."

They went out, shutting the heavy old door behind them, while Roy hastened into the bathroom, and dashed the clear, cold water over her face and arms. Coming back, a little later, she stood gazing wanly at her reflection in the green twilight of the mirror. I must get well soon, she thought, as she opened the top drawer and found powder and a comb and brush, and even a fresh lipstick. Timothy hasn't anybody but me . . . She leaned nearer, and ran the comb through her short, dark curls; I can't let anything happen to me. I am all he has to depend on . . . She carefully outlined the full, rich curve of her lips: I can't afford to die. I am obliged to get well . . .

Voices floated up from the dining-room, and when Roy entered, Craig turned on her, first a surprised glance, and then an arrested meditative gaze.

"You look different, Roy," she said. "You look rested."

Roy laughed. "You mean I look restored."

By the dining-room table Kate was pouring milk from a pitcher of palest blue Ridgeway ware, and, over a foamy stream, she talked to Timothy, who was seated in a baby's armchair, drumming with a spoon on a doll's table. His face was smeared with bread and milk, and he was wearing his rare blissful smile. With that smile, he is sure to have a good life, Roy said to herself.

"That was my armchair and my doll's table," Kate was saying. "Father had them made for me on my third Christmas." She gave Roy a glass of milk, and made her sit down near a plate of buttered bread, at the end of the table. "We haven't much to offer anybody," she said, "but there is always plenty of milk, and we make our own butter. Those eggs were laid this morning. I mashed up one for Timothy, and he asked for another."

"I am famished." Roy drank her milk, and held out her glass to be filled. "This milk tastes like sunshine." She added, with a sigh: "I feel as if I'd gone empty for weeks."

Kate broke the shell of an egg, and watched the girl while she ate. "You must have gone hungry, or you couldn't look so thin and wasted. But that's all over now. Farmers go shabby, but they don't go hungry, not so long as hens lay eggs, and cows give milk, and green stuff comes up in the garden."

"Goo! Goo! Good!" Timothy cried, thumping harder with the back of his spoon.

"Yes, darling," Roy answered, as she met Kate's look, so candid, so wide and free and tolerant in range. What has happened? she asked herself. Was it merely that she was no longer hungry? Or was the outward harmony of Kate's surroundings only a reflection of an inner reconciliation with life? Was it wisdom? Was it goodness? Or was it some rare physical adjustment, some equal measure of spirit and body? Kate's features were not unusual, Roy admitted; her figure, in the purple-blue cardigan, was almost shapeless; but there was a subdued radiance in her smile, and an autumn bloom lingered in her homely fresh-coloured face . . . No, the secret is not in what she is, Roy found herself thinking: The secret is in what she makes the rest of us feel.

"I am glad Daddy will not go back with me," she burst out, impulsively. "I am glad, even if I have to let Timothy go until I am well."

Kate turned to look at her, and suddenly, without knowing why, Roy felt that Kate was finding a way. "You will give him to us, dear. You will give him to us until you come back to live here. Do you think Asa's grandchild could go to a stranger?"

"Oh, but Daddy," Roy stammered. "Daddy didn't tell me."

"He left it to me. But he knew." Kate's voice was strong and gentle and comforting. "He knew, without anyone's telling him."

With a daze of light in her eyes, Roy looked up at her. "It is too much. Even now, you are working too hard. You never stop, Daddy says, as long as there is anything to be done . . . It wouldn't be fair."

Kate laughed. "There is never too much of the right thing. The way can always be found. After seeing Timothy, do you think I'd let him go to . . . to . . ."

"How will you manage?" Craig asked, knitting his eyebrows. "You are out of doors all day."

"Oh, we'll find a way. It will be easier in winter. By next spring, Roy may be here to look after him. When she comes back from her camp, we'll have the screened porch upstairs ready for her to sleep on, and she and Timothy may live on milk and eggs and butter."

Roy was weeping, silently, her face in her hands. What was the meaning of it? Has Kate anything that I have not, that Mother has not, that Aunt Charlotte, for all her generous instincts, has never felt? What was it that made Kate able to work her effortless miracles? Could one solitary human being, through goodness and wisdom alone, gather the broken fragments of other lives, and bind them together? Roy knew what people would say . . . all the people who did not believe in goodness, who did not know wisdom. Mother, she thought, will never forgive me. Even Aunt Charlotte, tolerant but obtuse, in her late-blooming selfishness, would mildly sorrow and disapprove. She could see the collective features of Queenborough, the aloof features of standards and traditions, of canons and precepts, of rubrics and rituals innumerable. She could see all these damaged yet impervious death-masks frozen in judgment. But none of these things mattered, while she choked back her sobs, and felt the tears wet her cheeks and leave the taste of salt on her lips . . .

From what seemed a vast distance, though it was, in reality, just under the staircase, the telephone rang without stopping. Steps crossed the hall; a door opened and shut; and she heard Craig's sharpened voice saying: "Hello! What? I can't get you. Yes. Yes, I hear you . . ." Then a pause, and again: "I will tell him. He will come as soon as I find him. Yes. Yes, I know. That is bad. I am sorry . . ."

Roy lifted her face, her eyes still shining with tears, and met Craig's guarded and inscrutable look. "That was Mrs. Fitzroy," he said. Your Mother has had a bad heart attack. She is asking for your father. But the doctor thinks she may not live till he comes . . ."

# PART THREE
## Evening: The Light in the Sky

# I

WHEN the afternoon softened and changed, a wing of pure gold swept down toward the west, and the whole sky was suddenly throbbing with light. In this light, the border of grasses by the river's edge stood out, separate and illuminated, against a blue background of water. Even the rusty crows skimming over a near cornfield reflected a brazen sheen.

Coming slowly along the path, Asa dropped on the bench Roy had left. He was more shaken by her return, he told himself, than he should have believed possible; and his eyes were blurred as he gazed after the receding figures on the upper terrace.

The shock was in his nerves, but beneath the shock and the stunned incredulity, he felt that this unknown child, facing an unknown world, had broken through his tranquility. Just as he had found himself anchored, in his sunny backwater, in this tideless peace of his later years, the memory of some long forgotten dilemma had risen again to confront him. For this child, with his clear eyes and his confident gaze, was different, he knew, was nearer, was more deeply related to his inner life, than were those other and older grandchildren, who belonged, not to him, but to the normal breed of Andrew and of Lavinia. How had he been able, he wondered, to hide both his shock and his surprised emotion, from Roy's questioning look? Yet he had hidden all these things, and he had hidden, too, the burning force of his resolve that never again would he allow himself to be drawn or driven back into the old habit of futile self-sacrifice.

But this child must be saved. Strangely enough, he found

117

that he was thinking less of Roy than of Timothy, which was, of course, only another way of thinking of Roy . . . He felt happy, yet curiously spent and exhausted. Not nervously tired, he told himself, because working in the earth was not like that old grinding job in the tobacco factory. But he was glad the day's tasks were not ended. After Roy left, he would keep on until well after dark, and while he was putting things in order and feeding the stock, his detached mind could work out its own problems. The part he liked best was the care of the horses. They were good companions, and he enjoyed looking after them. He imagined farm life was more human and friendly in the long, slow ages, when farmers walked up and down the furrows, after a horse and a plough, and the cows, with sad or cheerful bells, came strolling home to be milked by the human touch, not by the indifferent power of electricity . . . Jack, he recalled, would order every new invention he could afford; but Asa was glad he had not turned Hunter's Fare into a model farm. It was fortunate that Kate had kept only enough cows, fine Jerseys all, to supply them with milk, cream, and butter. That would be good, he thought, disconnectedly, for the growing boy. Kate would find a way, he knew, to keep the little chap on the farm. Overworked as she was, he couldn't ask her; but he had learned, in the past few years, that problems might be safely left to Kate's generous impulses . . . If ever a man had needed and found a friend . . .

As the gay evening wind tossed the branches, the rippling willow-leaves turned and whitened, and broke into a lacy foam. If only the weather holds, he thought, dreamily. This weather is like happiness. Through the farthest trunks of the willows, he could see the oldest part of the apple orchard, with piles of bright red apples heaped under the boughs. Many of the trees bore only imperfect fruit, but Kate insisted that the blossoms in spring were better than apples.

While he rested there, in the hushed life of the hour, warmed by the sun, and by the bitter-sweet tang of autumn, it seemed to him that he was caught and held in some slow drift of time. Barred with a pattern of light and shade, the terraces appeared to rise and fall, and to settle back, silently, under the blown grass. Within this stillness, the wind moved, the grass bent and straightened, the fall of leaves broke and scattered. All these separate motions were imprisoned here, now, in the crystal globe of this instant. But, beyond this sphere of eternity, above, below, around the encircled moment, he felt that changeless, perpetual rhythm of time passing. Clouds and light, air and water, tree and flower, all were drifting. Even the wild geese, ranging far overhead, through the bright hollow of afternoon, appeared to float, like shadows, in a liquid medium. For it was the closing season of an abundant earth, when nature, serene and effortless, was drifting into the long pause of winter . . .

A voice called, and he started up. Awaking from his sleep, which was not sleep, he remembered that outside this stillness, this peace, this crystal globe, the retarded evolution of men had turned back on itself, and was, even now, devouring its own children.

From the upper terrace, Roy was running down to him. As she approached, he saw her image, first indistinctly, through a shower of leaves, and then, more clearly, as a disturbed and hurrying figure. The wind rumpled her hair and outlined her too slender shape beneath the thin folds of her dress. He tried to put speed into his dragging walk, but his legs had grown stiff in the muscles, and presently he was obliged to stop and draw his breath while she came up with him.

"It's turning colder, Roy," he said anxiously. "With that cough you should be careful."

She brushed his warning aside. "Oh, Daddy, they think

Mother is dying. She has asked for you, but she may not last till you come."

For an instant, while he looked at her, he breathed more heavily. But all he said was, "I'll go. You said she asked for me?"

"The doctor thinks we may be too late."

"You will go with me?" As they walked on, he put his arm about her. "Craig can do my work tonight and tomorrow. Are you cold, darling?"

"No, I'm warm inside. Mrs. Oliver is going to take Timothy till I'm well again . . . and, oh, Daddy, she says we may live here."

"I know, dear. I thought she would." He pressed her closer, and sighed, as he felt her thinness and frailty. "I don't know how Kate does so much without showing the strain. I suppose it is because she takes everything smoothly and lightly, as if none of this external bother were really important. Good or bad, she never makes a fuss about living."

"I never dreamed what she was like," Roy answered. "Mother said . . ." She caught back her words, and continued, "Then I may leave him here."

"What else can you do? He'll like the farm, and we'll like having him. Kate will scour the county till she finds a good woman to look after him while she is at work."

They quickened their steps, and he said, hurriedly, when they reached the porch, "It won't take me but a minute to change. Will you tell Craig to bring round the truck?"

"There is the station wagon. I suppose he thought it would be easier on you. Or, perhaps . . ."

"That's right, dear. I'll be down by the time you're ready."

"Oh, poor Mother! Is it really so bad as they think?"

"God knows, my dear. She has pulled through some bad attacks. What was it you used to say of her: She always wins the last battle."

"I wish she'd had a better life, Daddy. I wish she'd ever, ever been happy. I wish," she broke off into tears, "I wish I could care more."

"I know, dear. Well, we'll start as soon as we can." After a sympathetic pat, he hastened ahead of her into the hall and upstairs to his room, where he found Kate had laid out clean clothes and his best suit. The hot water was already running in the tub; and as he dashed into the bathroom, he called out: "It won't take me many minutes." Even in her last moments, Lavinia would feel mortified by a husband who had come from the fields, and was still wearing overalls. Her final scene—if this were final—must be set in the great tradition of manners. While he hastily splashed in soapy water, dried his steaming body, and dressed himself with stumbling fingers, he heard, in his harassed mind, a faint recurring echo of Roy's cry: "I wish she'd ever been happy! I wish I could care more!" Yet the next instant, he admitted, philosophically, that caring was independent alike of reason and of will, that love had always been, and would remain, a rebel emotion. I gave what I could, he thought. It was not her fault, and it was not mine, that we never really liked each other. For they had never liked each other less than in those few hectic months when they had believed themselves to be in love . . .

In the front hall, Kate was waiting for him, with a replenished pitcher of milk. "Drink this, Asa, and eat a few sandwiches. You may not have any supper." He felt her quiet strength, and he thought: This is her power. She rules circumstances because she has learned to rule her own mind.

"Your overcoat is in the wagon." She waited until he had eaten a sandwich and finished a glass of milk. "Have you everything you could need?"

"Everything. Can you manage with just Craig to help you? I'll try to be back in the morning."

"Don't worry. We can manage. Take your time about coming down." Kate turned to Roy. "Won't you let me keep Timothy?"

Roy shook her head. "We'll take him. I left his clothes, unpacked, in my old room. But, tomorrow, Father will bring him back to you." While she answered, she was hurriedly slipping on the child's jacket, and making him ready for the long drive. A minute later, when they ran out of the door, she looked over her shoulder, as if she were leaving a place that she loved. "Good-bye. You have been wonderful to me." Her voice choked and she swallowed a sob. "You will never know . . . I can never tell you how grateful I feel." Then, while Timothy nestled at her side, and the station wagon sped through rippling masses of light and shade, she added aloud: "I don't know what it is that makes her so . . . so . . ."

"I've asked myself that question," Asa replied slowly. "Sometimes, I think it is because . . . oh, well, because she is the least negative person I have ever known. She has never lost a strong emotion toward life. I wonder what this world would become if there were more like her."

Roy sighed. "I always thought beauty and charm were the two best gifts for a woman. But there's something still better." After a pause, she asked doubtfully, "Do you suppose Mother would call her a good woman?"

"Perhaps not." There was a sparkle of merriment in his glance. "Do you know, my dear, I have a feeling that your mother will pull through this attack."

"So have I," Roy assented. "She has had so many heart spasms. Aunt Charlotte thinks Mother will outlive us all."

"Well, I hope so. Even if she has not been happy, in her way, she has been able to enjoy unhappiness. She gets a good deal out of life, especially," there was an edge to his tone, "since I deserted her."

As he answered, he could feel the relief that surged over Roy. In spite of her smothered resentment, he knew, sympathetically, that she could not bear to think of a world without the solid, and often disturbing fact of a home, however unhappy, and of a mother, however exasperating. Death is always frightening to the young, and inherited family feeling, he told himself, prefers an obstacle to a vacuum. The conflict would go on; but, even if Roy hated her, Lavinia's child would still wish to keep her mother alive.

"Then I'll feel safe and happy, Daddy. Nobody is going to die, and Timothy will be with you and Mrs. Oliver. And Mrs. Oliver is almost a stranger," she broke off with a laugh, "but strangers are kind . . ."

There was a mellow light on the road. The long shadows, falling crosswise, were driven by the purple mist from the river. Beyond a field of shocked corn and a narrow glimmer of burnished water, a dark ball of fire was slowly sinking toward the western horizon.

"Strangers . . ." Asa repeated, vaguely, and stopped. He was thinking of that stranger whose face he had never seen, yet who would live on, unrecognized, in the grandchild, at Hunter's Fare. He hoped the boy would turn to the land, that he would prove to be a natural-born farmer, as Asa himself was, though he had spent the better part of his life in a factory. But the inner rhythm stirred somewhere, in his unconscious depths. His hidden dream had moved among the eternal aspects of nature, obeying the elemental gestures of sowing and reaping. "And it came true," he murmured, with his eyes on the white road ahead. "My dream came to life in the end."

"What did you say, Daddy?"

"I don't know, darling. I was wondering, I think, about the boy. Did his father have those blue eyes?"

"I can't remember, Daddy," Roy's tone was expressionless. "They were light eyes, I know, but that is all. He had a bad scar, and that made him try to keep his face turned away. And the room, too, was dark . . . not really dark, but there was only one shaded lamp, and the storm gave a queer murkiness to everything. It is all like a nightmare that you remember in daylight."

"Yes, I see. I see. And his hair . . . Was his hair that golden colour?"

"No, it was light chestnut. I can remember that, and the thick way it sprang up from his head. But it was very light, not dark, chestnut. It may have looked golden in daylight."

How remote those hours had become, to her, Asa thought, how remote, and impersonal, and unreal. She could speak of that night as if it were a scene she had watched on the stage. It appeared to be withdrawn and unrelated to the thinnest thread of emotion. Does she really feel so little? he asked himself, wonderingly. Has she forgotten—or pretended to forget—that unknown man's relationship to the flesh and blood figure of Timothy?

While he was thinking this, Roy pressed nearer and laid her hand on his arm. "I want him to be like you, Daddy. Won't you try to make him like you?"

Without shifting his gaze from the road, Asa shook his head in denial. "You haven't heard what they are saying in Queenborough . . . Is Timothy awake or asleep?"

"Oh, I know, I know . . . They see only the outside of things. They believe in appearances . . . He is fast asleep on my arm."

"That is the safe way, my child. The world needs safety first."

"I despise people who are thinking always of safety."

"How did that help you, Roy?"

"Not the very least bit. But I still despise playing for safety. Mother and Aunt Charlotte are being safe when they refuse to take Timothy."

Asa smiled. "Your mother is a noble figure, my child. She has lived up to her ideals. Never forget that. I hope," he added, more gravely, "this illness is no worse than her other heart failures."

They had left the shocked corn far behind, and, over the level fields in the distance, a thin green veil of winter wheat reflected the reddish glow of the sunset. "Oh, I hope," Roy agreed, but he could see that her mind was still occupied with Timothy's future. "I do want him to be like you, Daddy," she continued, after a moment. "I want him to have whatever it is that has held you together after . . . after you seemed to have lost everything."

"My dear, you are mistaken in me. I had nothing. I was born with a sense of failure . . . of incompleteness. Or, perhaps, this was driven into me as a child . . . All on earth I had to hold by was . . . oh, well, I suppose you may call it a buried dream. I thought that dream was dead at the end. No man was more surprised than I when it came alive."

"But you had more than that. Even if you didn't know it, you had something more, Daddy. I learned this when I tried to break away from you. A strange doctor taught me, then, that your life must have a root . . . a living root, somewhere. They brought him to see me in the hospital. I think they feared, or hoped, I was turning into a mental case. I was so low in my mind . . . He told me, that doctor, I had the sickness—or would he have said, disease?—of civilization. He said we were all trying to escape from our roots in nature . . . in the simple goodness of living. And he said, too, we could only run round and round, in a circle, until we edged nearer a precipice, or came back to win or to lose the fight within ourselves . . . Of course, I can't remember his words. But this was what he meant. This was when I began to see that my help could not come from outside . . . that it must come from my very own self . . . But I never forget that my deepest roots are in you, Daddy."

"My dear, my dear . . ."

"Don't laugh at me, Daddy. It meant so much. Just seeing the mistakes I'd made."

"Mistakes are our common heritage, my child. But your mother has never torn up her roots. She has grown deeper."

"In tradition. But hasn't her tradition always been a delusion of . . . well, of superiority? I suppose that was her way of escape."

"Perhaps." He smiled grimly, and the next instant his face softened. "Well, I'm glad you found your way home, darling. I'm glad you've come back to us."

She shook her head. "To you, not to the others. I can't feel as they do, but I must believe in something outside myself. I want to hold by something good, not only for myself, but for Timothy. That is why I am holding to you, Daddy."

His eyes were moist as he glanced at her, and then quickly back to the road. "Wait till you see how they feel about me tonight. You are holding not to me, dear, but to your own inner strength. It was always there . . . And, I suppose, what we are, not what we appear to be or what we do, shapes our lives in the end . . ."

His voice stopped, and for miles they drove slowly, in silence. Hours before—or so it seemed to him—the ball of dark fire had split apart, and the fragments had burned out along the western horizon. Later, the pale greenish afterglow had dissolved into mist, and the shining windows of houses were scattered, near and far, over the landscape. Then, at last, as they went on, the spires and roofs of the city started out, in a sudden flare, against the screen of the night.

# II

A s the station wagon shot up a steep hill, and descended by a winding road on the other side, they were swept into the bedraggled outskirts of Queenborough. On the left, an overgrown bank fell abruptly toward the antiquated jail and the huddled quarter known as Jail Alley. But an immense space, both visible and invisible, divided this part of town from the rows of closely built houses, some neat, some untidy, which straggled along the high street on the top of the next hill. There were brief lawns in front of these houses, with doormat gardens, in which late summer flowers were still bearing their sad blossoms. From every door or gate, fathers and mothers, carrying lunch-boxes, were setting out to their night's work in the defense plants or factories; and after them, as they turned down the hill, bands of infant destructives streamed, restlessly, on adventures of darkness. By midnight the bolder gangs might be caught up in a far-flung police-net, while the more timid natures scurried, like frightened mice, back to shelter. "This is the free children's hour," Asa said grimly, watching a small, determined girl, in boy's clothes, viciously digging a fox-hole in the midst of an absent neighbour's flower-bed.

"Is it the war fever?" Roy asked, and added, thoughtfully: "I hope it will be over before Timothy grows bigger."

"I hope so," Asa repeated, abstractedly. "After all, these wild innocents must build our better world if it comes. Of such stuff, we must make peace and freedom."

"They aren't all like these, Daddy. There are others . . ." She glanced down at the sleeping child.

"Yes, the unknown. We must trust to that. But isn't it our nature to long for peace and freedom, even while we destroy them?" His tone changed. "I shall leave the station wagon outside, and start back by daybreak. Craig will have to bring the truck with the machinery."

"But if Mother is really so ill?"

"Then I'll telephone Craig, and stay as long as I can. I'd like to put you on your train tomorrow morning."

"How did Mrs. Oliver ever manage without you?"

"Well, she had the old overseer. That was before the war."

Roy sighed. "I suppose the farm means more to you than anything else."

He nodded. "In a way, yes. What means most to a man, I think, is having a part in life."

So this was what life and the war meant, Roy thought. To find something more important than living or dying, or than one's own peculiar happiness or unhappiness. "Oh, Daddy," she said, "I wish I had been different. I wish I had known better."

His smile shone on her, tender and understanding, yet always tinctured with irony. "I rather like you as you are."

In the gathering obscurity, the huddled roofs of the city rolled past them. Lights flickered and disappeared, and flickered again. When the white glare flashed over his profile, the fine, clear contour looked as if it were graven in some transparent medium. Little was said on the way through the traffic; and while they sat, side by side, a single impression flowed from Asa to Roy, and then back, once more, to dart off in an unrelated sequence of thought . . . Are we really living two lives, the true and the false? How long ago had they stepped on that bit of earth, which was Westward Avenue, and turned homeward together, down the long block, with their shadows running slantwise under the street lamps? Everything was different, now, yet nothing had changed—nothing but their inner world and time passing, which had streamed through that world and swept over its boundaries. And around them, the night and the city seemed to fall apart, and then to move on again into the next instant, the next happening, the next hour or day.

"Yes, if your mother is better, I must go back immediately," Asa was saying. "I must be back on the farm by tomorrow."

Not until they approached the end of the block, and noticed that several cars were waiting in front of the lighted house, were they startled into a comprehension of danger. Then, while Asa picked up the child, and they hurried across the pavement, they saw the door swing open, slowly and mournfully.

For one breathless instant, Asa felt, beneath his shaken will, a sudden violent surge in some dark chaos of mind. Has it come at last . . . freedom? The involuntary cry rose, and sank, and died in the unconscious depths.

"Oh, poor Mother," Roy was sobbing. "She was really so ill, and I didn't believe it." Her voice faltered with pity.

Framed in the doorway, regarding them with the chill courtesy and the suppressed hostility of affronted convention, a handsome elderly lady waited for them to enter the hall. They both knew her; they had known her all their lives; for she was Louisa Littlepage, Lavinia's closest friend, and, in Queenborough, the last indomitable champion of the reforming conscience. Under the dim light, she appeared to be carved, not from yielding flesh, but from some worn yet unbreakable substance of character. The even ridges of her iron-gray hair were unstirred by the opening door. Her narrow feet, firmly planted on the flattest of heels, were immovable. "You are too late, Mr.

Timberlake. Your wife asked for you when she felt the end was approaching." A white flower dropped from her hands, and she stooped to pick it up from the carpet.

"I came as soon as I heard." As the reply passed Asa's lips, it seemed to him that the lofty towers of his freedom toppled over, and fell, and were scattered in ruins. If Louisa Littlepage represented the forces of prejudice, under which he had suffered, she embodied also a moral order that might be defeated, but would not ever surrender.

She made, now, a vague and tolerant gesture, while her gaze rested, with obvious pity, on the child in his arms. "Lavinia asked me to care for the little boy."

"Not now." Asa held Timothy tighter.

"I thought you would wish to see her . . . She passed on as she had lived. There was no bitterness in her heart. There was only forgiveness for all she had suffered."

So there was no escape from his marriage. After the tyranny, in life, of Lavinia's virtue, he was now condemned to bear, in death, the heavier burden of her magnanimity. She had won, yet again and ultimately, the last battle.

The child was beginning to whimper. Behind him, as they ascended the stairs, he could hear Roy sobbing: "Poor Mother. I didn't know. I wouldn't believe she was dying."

This is regret, Asa thought. It is easier for some of us to escape from love than from regret. Slow footsteps moved overhead, while he felt that the very breath of the house was suspended and withdrawn in aversion.

When they reached the top of the staircase, a door opened and closed, and opened again, as Charlotte's shapeless figure appeared and stopped short at the sight of them. Tears were already drying on her mottled cheeks; for her self-indulgent emotions, so long suppressed, would gush forth at the slightest excuse, and purge her large, flat mind of restraint.

"You came too late." There was a rasping catch in her voice.

"I know. I am sorry." What could he do but repeat empty syllables?

"She asked for you. The end came soon after we reached you."

"I know."

With an embarrassed gesture, as if she were speaking aloud in church, Charlotte put her hand over her mouth, and turning her disarranged head, coughed delicately. "I wish you could have been here. At first, the pain was distressing. Then, after the doctor came, and gave two injections, she fell asleep."

"Yes, yes, I know."

"She spoke beautifully of you." For a quickly repressed instant, Charlotte's natural worldliness broke through. "Louisa and the nurse have just left her. They wanted you to see her as you remembered her . . . before . . . before . . ."

So soon, Asa thought, and then, but was it really so soon?

"I can never be too thankful for Louisa." Charlotte's words burst out with a gasping sob. "She has attended to everything. I cannot tell you what she has spared me. She and the nurse together have arranged it all. Louisa had brought her some flowers only this morning. It has been a lesson to me, the way Louisa put aside her own grief, and took immediate charge of. . . of . . ."

"Yes. Yes, she met us downstairs."

"I felt I never really understood Lavinia." After a quivering effort, Charlotte recovered her breath and spoke again with her soft huskiness. "Until she passed away, I never knew what was in her nature . . . how much beauty—how much fortitude. I feel that she was the last of—of a noble tradition."

But Mrs. Littlepage will carry on . . . Though the words formed in Asa's mind, they were bitten back by his teeth. Aloud, he said only, "May I go in now?"

"And you, too, Roy." Charlotte stepped aside from the threshold. "Though your father may wish to be alone with her. She may still have her message." She stretched out large benevolent arms. "Give me the child. Louisa is waiting downstairs for the—the . . ." Her tongue tripped over a word, and she babbled on, in confusion, "for Mr. Smithson . . ."

Yes, Louisa and the nurse had done their part. There was a single candle and a vase of flowers at Lavinia's head, and they had slipped on her best pale lavender bed-jacket. Her closed eyes and the smooth planes of her face were expressionless, but there was an expectant air in her composed attitude, as if she were waiting, while she rested, to receive important visitors. So soon, Asa thought again, and, more slowly, with a kind of shocked surprise: Must death, like life, wait on appearances?

He heard the door close, and his hand reached out for Roy, who stood by his side. For some minutes, she stayed there, without moving; then, withdrawing her hand from his clasp, she turned away from him and went, noiselessly, out of the room.

What is there in death, he found himself thinking, even when we admit neither its grief nor its urgency, that puts a clutch on the heart or the nerves? He could not mourn for Lavinia. He could not, with truth, tell his shrinking mind, that he regretted his freedom. Yet, standing there, he could feel the loss of a power more vast than any single identity. Charlotte was right, he thought. Finality had touched Lavinia's commonplace features with the grave outline of legend. Her death had become, for the moment, if but for the moment alone, the death of a tradition. Not ever in life had she worn that aspect of high detachment, of effortless dignity. His gaze, earnest and seeking, rested on the bluish hollows in her temples, on the delicate arches above her eyelids. He had seen her always as a plain and ordinary woman, without charm or loveliness, but, as he looked down on her vacant features, she appeared innocent and ennobled.

From without, through the wide-open window, floated the harsh discord, now high, now low, now near, now far away, of thickening night over the city. Still farther off, he heard or felt the broken tumult of a world dying in conflict. Yet was it, in truth, a dying world? Or only a blind and deluded epoch in history? For it seemed to him, at the moment, that an era, as well as a tradition, was ending. And not an era alone, but a bright, lost vision, a long adventure, an inaccessible hope. All the outward forms which had designed, and illumined, and circumscribed, and finally destroyed the pattern of his life, all these, with their many changing shapes, were now over. Yet something, he felt, without words, was still left, something, if only the living seeds of tomorrow. The past, in its high beauty and its low cruelty, in its perpetual seeking and finding, or seeking and not finding, this past, he told himself, still lingered there, out in the night, beyond the farthest shadow of that dark violence. Other worlds, related or unrelated, would take shape and emerge. Other worlds and other dreams, and, in time perhaps, other ruins of worlds and dreams . . .

A hand closed over his, and he heard the quivering murmur of Roy's voice. "Poor Mother. Oh, but, Daddy, I wouldn't believe she was dying. I feel as if I were to blame for . . . for it all."

"I know, my dear. There isn't a bit of reason in it, not the least bit. I know it isn't true, yet, somehow—I don't know why —I feel that way myself."

Roy wiped her eyes and bent over Lavinia. "She looks happy, but she had so little in life."

"She had more than you know. She had her world."

"And that, too, is going. It may be a blessing that she died with all she believed in. When everything we have known is gone, what will be left to us?"

Asa looked past her, through the window, where, above the church spires and the huddled roofs, the luminous wing of a searchlight was sweeping the sky. Together, they gazed upward, while the last faint glimmer sank and faded into the unconquerable darkness beyond. "We have the unknown," he answered, slowly. "We have ourselves."

There was a slight, groping push at his side, and he asked, without turning. "What is it, Roy?" Then, as Roy did not reply, he glanced down and saw that the child had slipped in, and stood gazing without fear, but with solemn, uninterested eyes at the still form on the bed. For an instant, while Asa watched him, Timothy remained mute and incurious. Then, suddenly, he stretched out his small empty hand. "B'ead? Budder?" he asked, pleadingly, and once again, when no answer came, he repeated, with impatient hunger: "B'ead!"

"He has not forgotten," Roy whispered. "She gave him a piece of bread. That is all she will ever mean to him."

That is all, Asa assented dumbly. That is the past, but the future still rests with us. The world without end is only the unattained and the unfulfilled in ourselves. And the illusion of security is the betrayal of man's hope on earth. Well, no matter. One learns that much from heartbreak . . .

"I couldn't hear, Daddy. What were you saying?"

"Nothing, my child. All you heard was on old fogey welcoming the unknown. An old fogey, past and gone, nothing more. But Timothy is the future, and for the future, the unknown is the heart of life."

While they stood there, the winged light again pierced the shadows and swept, unerringly, across the wide arch of sky.

*BEYOND DEFEAT*

was composed, printed, and bound by
Kingsport Press, Inc., Kingsport, Tennessee.
The paper is Warren's Novel Antique. The
types are Electra, Garamont, Nicholas Cochin,
and Centaur. The book was designed by
John J. Walklet, Jr.